Willy's Ballgame

Copyright © Dennis Ricci, 2011. All rights reserved. No part of this book may be reproduced or transmitted in any form or by any means, electronic or mechanical, including photocopying, recording, or by any information storage and retrieval system, without permission in writing from the publisher.
"Working My Way Back to You", Music and Lyrics by Sandy Linzer and Denny Randall, Copyright (C) 1966.
"Jimmy Mack", Music and Lyrics by Eddie Holland, Lamont Dozier, and Brian Holland. Copyright (C) 1967.

Bedside Books
An imprint of American Book Publishing
5442 So. 900 East, #146
Salt Lake City, UT 84117-7204
www.american-book.com
Printed in the United States of America on acid-free paper.

Willy's Ballgame

Designed by Swat Geracymchuk, design@american-book.com

Publisher's Note: This is a work of fiction. Names, characters, places, and incidents either are the product of the author's imagination, or are used fictitiously, and any resemblance to actual persons, living or dead, events, or locales is entirely coincidental.

ISBN-13: 978-1-58982-833-9
ISBN-10: 1-58982-833-X

Ricci, Dennis, Willy's Ballgame

Special Sales

These books are available at special discounts for bulk purchases. Special editions, including personalized covers, excerpts of existing books, and corporate imprints, can be created in large quantities for special needs. For more information e-mail info@american-book.com.

Willy's Ballgame

By Dennis Ricci

Dedication

To Denise, Leigh, Chris, and Casey, who braided Willy's pigtails before every game and told her to sing "The Star Spangled Banner" out loud at the World Series.

Prologue

Willy Mae Beal was on fire inside the pitcher's circle in Oklahoma City at the College Softball Championship Tournament. She was pitching for Florida A&M in the semifinal against the University of Connecticut.

"This is the third team of Huskies we've taken on this season," she said to Jenny Posey, her roommate, teammate, and battery mate. "Northeastern, Washington State, and now UConn. The doggie logos get kind of tired after a while, don't they?"

"Believe it," Willy replied, unsmiling. She was panning the crowd for a familiar face. Her grandfather promised to make the trip and her mother bought him his ticket, but Willy hadn't spied him yet. Then she zeroed in on the laughing eyes, the little grin, and the almost shy wave of his gnarled, arthritic hand.

"Hey, Papp," Willy whispered from afar. "Willy loves you."

Willy turned her attention to matters at hand: a new inning and the batter stepping into the box. The face in the crowd was Reuben Henry. Rube was seated alongside another elder gent, Amos Jones, lifelong friend, long-time rival, and sometime teammate.

"We played ball *together*," they said, although they spent more time on different teams, trying to best each other, than the occasional wayside stop at which they put on the same uniform. The names of their teams are all but forgotten: Washington Senators, Oakland Oaks, Homestead Grays, and Kansas City Monarchs.

Rube Henry and Amos "Teach" Jones were part of an almost-lost generation of ballplayers, old enough to have played in the shadow leagues of the "blackball" era and young enough to have had a taste of life on the green pastures of big league baseball, but unable to enjoy a full career among the elite where they always belonged. Whenever they got together, now less often in their twilight years, they called the roll.

"I can't believe poor old Campy's gone," Amos began.

"Satch is gone," Rube continued.

"Spahnie's gone."

"Double-D, Don Drysdale."

"Jamie, ninety-some years old and died within a few days of his wife," pronounced Amos, referring to James "Cool Papa" Bell by the name Jamie, as only intimates knew him.

"Ted and Joe, both gone!" declared Rube.

"The Mick was just a kid and Roger Maris, too!"

"Josh Gibson wasn't even thirty-five, playin' with a brain tumor 'til it killed him."

"Seems to me Josh and Lou Gehrig started a whole thing of good men dyin' young. Remember Gil Hodges and Jackie Robinson dyin' right about the same time?"

"What killed Jackie Robinson was *bein'* Jackie Robinson," posited Rube.

"He lost a son," Amos countered solemnly. "You don't get over that."

"I wonder . . . "

"Who's next?"

"Probably me!" Rube thumped two fingers on his chest.

"Ticker?" asked Amos, who watched Rube nod and reach for a hot dog, fries, and a sudsy beer from a cardboard box between his feet. "You know, that don't help matters none."

Rube flipped his hand dismissively and gestured toward Florida A&M's pitcher. "That li'l gal there and her mama would have me eatin' nothin' but carrots and celery and apple sauce. Like to kill me before I'm even dead!"

Amos laughed mightily. "That little girl is one tall drink of water. What is she, six foot and then some?"

"Six-foot-two," Rube said. He turned, obviously with painful effort, toward his friend, whom he invited to meet him at this particular event and venue—a good excuse—midway between their respective homes in Florida and California. "Did y'all really drive all the way out here?"

"I like to," Amos said. "It reminds me of the old days, ridin' them buses, lookin' out the window, lookin' at nothin'."

"I flew on some cheap airline," said Rube as he chewed through a mouthful of meat and bun. "How's your Louise doin'?"

Amos's eyes narrowed sadly. "Since the stroke, she's helpless as a baby. We're all gettin' old." One man's weathered hand closed upon the other's. "How old you be now?" Amos asked Rube.

"Eighty-one come August the eighteenth."

"Uh-huh, you're still older than me, Rube."

"Would appear so!" chuckled Rube.

"Say, this here's a *game*." When Amos said it that way, he

meant a *good* game.

"Nothin' to nothin' with two down in the fifth," Rube announced.

"Now, I don't want to jinx her, but . . . "

"She's workin' on a no-hitter."

"Perfect game," Amos added.

"And more than that." Rube removed the penciled scorebook from under his arm and held it open to reveal a continuous column of kays. "Fourteen batters and fourteen strikeouts . . . pretty maids all in a row!"

"She *is* good," quoted Amos. "These young girls are *all* good. Aren't they, Rube?"

"They hit and run, bunt, and be stealin' bases. They use their legs and their heads. These gals play like we used to back in our day."

The old-timers' loose-lipped defiance of the time-honored jinx—one never mentions a no-hitter in progress—had less to do with what happened next than the batter at the plate, UConn's pitcher, Marie Elaina Rios. A tough-talking barrio girl, she was short and stocky, the physical antithesis of Willy Beal. Yet they were alike in their parallel mental and physical competitiveness. Marie Elaina studied her opposite number's every move—her alternating windmill and slingshot deliveries, her fastball, her "drop," her "rise," and her marginally legal straight-armed slider that spun along a slightly arced trajectory, then dropped abruptly, smack-dab on home plate, usually evading a swinging bat.

"Can you hit her?" the Huskies' coach had asked.

"Hit her?" Marie Elaina was incredulous. "I can't even *see* the freakin' ball, coach."

Instead she would "work" the opposing pitcher. The tall girl's fast windmill beat Marie Elaina twice for two strikes, but

Willy's offspeed and breaking pitches fell out of the strike zone. The pitcher at the plate never lifted the bat off her shoulder until Willy uncorked a high-speed sizzler. The hitter stuck out her bat and slapped it away–foul. The next serve came in slower and higher and she chopped it into the dirt. The two women gritted their teeth and fixed their gaze on each other's eyes. Willy's next pitch on a full count sailed over the plate, knee high. Both women held their breath as the umpire muttered, "Take your base."

Amos and Rube watched Willy spit, prance about, and kick divots in the dirt of the grassless, "skinned" infield.

"I can hear them cuss words all the way up here, Rube."

"It's a good thing her mama stayed home."

The next UConn Husky to bat swung three times in terrified self-defense at pitches nearer to her head than the plate, thus ending the inning.

"She's always been that way. Since she was six years old and she hounded me to bring her to sign up for a pee-wee league, even though she was somethin' like two years too young." Rube made a fist and pressed it to his midsection. "She's got the fire in her belly."

"Just like us," Amos added.

"How're them boys of yours doin', Teach?"

"James," Amos replied, "he's finished now. He's bound and determined to stay in the game somehow, though. He married a nice Irish girl from up in Canada. They give us a new grand kid just about every year. He never really made the big bucks. They're broke . . . and happy as two pigs in a poke."

"And Peter, the younger one?"

"All the talent in the world and no discipline!"

Rube laughed and said, "That young buck collected a

bushel full of taters last season."

"Fifty-one," Amos touted proudly. "When he went on a home run spree in August, I thought he had a shot at breakin' the record. Then in September . . . *nothin'!*"

"Ain't that always the way?" Rube sang.

Amos tapped his forehead. "My boy Peter's a smart sonofagun, too. Not just baseball smart . . . makes more money in a year than I ever made in my whole life! He's got himself stocks, bonds, IRAs, CDs, all that stuff . . . and he married a pretty woman with brains to boot."

"Speakin' of which . . . " Rube gestured toward the A&M Lady Rattlers' bench, where Willy stood helmeted with bat in hand, talking to her coach, Jerry Wilkinson.

"It looks like you have to do it yourself, kiddo." Willy cast her eyes at her cleats and flipped the strands of her beaded braids over her shoulder. "We're in the top of the seventh, the last inning. The beginning of the end . . . "

"Or the end of the beginning," she quipped flippantly.

Jerry's eyes widened. "Stay focused, Willy." She nodded and looked him in the eye. "Get on base. Get into scoring position. If you can get to third, we'll go for a safety squeeze."

"Gotcha, coach!"

Without pretense of swinging away, Willy deftly moved her bat to the ball and dropped a bricklike bunt flat on the ground, less than three feet from the catcher. By the time the backstop unmasked, picked up the ball, and uncorked a throw, Willy had breezed safely past first base.

Amos marveled, "She runs as fast as she throws."

"Pretty near," Rube concurred, feeling no small measure of pride for the almost grownup woman-child he loved more than anyone else in his fully lived lifetime.

Willy crouched with one foot off the bag and trained her vision on the pitcher. The instant Husky Rios released the ball, Willy bolted to second and beat the catcher's throw standing up. On the next pitch, the catcher's throw was quicker and right on the money. Willy leaned to her left before pushing off and sliding into the bag, under the infielder's tag. Willy turned toward Jenny, wielding her bat at the plate. Jenny was the kind of player who would spit on a catcher's shoes, then kick dirt in her face when she looked down to see what happened. There would be none of that now. Her job was simple. Hit the ball so that Willy could score.

Willy drew blood as she bit down on her tongue, trying hard to hold herself back from "deeking." If she lifted her back foot before the pitcher released the ball, she would be called out for leaving the base too soon. She took a deep breath, eyes shut, exhaling the words, "There's no place like home."

The infielders at first and third played close, halfway up the line, their open gloves touching the ground and their free hands poised to trap anything hit their way. Willy watched Marie Elaina's arm come around and waited for her fingers to flutter. Willy flew home and Jenny punched the ball just to the right of the pitcher. Willy launched herself over the hunched catcher with an arm applied to her back, propelling an end-over-end rolling tumble. Willy sucked up a mouthful of dirt and her face scraped the plate. "Safe!" The score stood at 1-0.

Moments later, Willy's coach and teammates surrounded her in the pitcher's circle. They connected solemnly, hands clasped, arms interlaced. "One run," said coach Jerry. "If we hold 'em, we get USC, the Lady Trojans, tomorrow, for all

Willy's Ballgame

the marbles. Whatever happens, I love you guys. Now, let's do it."

Nine female softballers yelled, "Yeah!" in unison and Willy's eyes opened to Jerry's staring straight at her. At first, she thought he wanted to say something, but he just tossed her the ball without a word.

Willy worked carefully, mostly offspeed, trying to draw batted balls for the fielders to put into play. The results were two batters out and two runners on base with her nemesis coming to bat. This time Marie Elaina ripped a clean hit into the outfield. Again, Willy kicked the dirt and stomped around the infield.

"Chill out, girlfriend!" Jenny implored from behind the plate.

"Keep your head in the game, Willy," her coach spoke far out of earshot.

The ex-big leaguer's grandchild fired one, two, three windmill fastballs, upwards of seventy-five miles an hour from a distance of forty-five feet, and watched the aluminum cylinder fly from the batter's hands for strike three. Willy whipped off her visor and leaped into the air only to fall back to earth in stunned silence. The umpire ruled interference. The bat had grazed Jenny's catcher's mitt before slipping from the batter's fingers. The runners advanced unchallenged and the game was tied, 1-1.

Willy tried to swallow her rage, but couldn't let it go. Endorphin overload and smoldering anger took hold of her. She delivered the final pitch of the game squarely between the next batter's shoulder blades. *Plunk!* The Lady Rattlers lost, 2-1.

"She's gonna be moanin' and groanin' about that interference call all summer long 'til school starts back up," lamented Rube with a sour face.

Willy was saying, "I lost it. I blew it. We lost because I lost it," as she cried in a sandwich embrace of her teammates in the locker room.

"She's young, Rube," Amos consoled his old compatriot. "There's always another game. Just like us!"

For Willy Beal, however, pitching another game like this one would be pure fantasy.

Also viewing the women's college softball semifinals from a hotel room on the outskirts of Denver, via rebroadcast on late-night cable, was Peter Jones. The son of Amos, an all-star and MVP award winner, labored in futility through eight hitless at-bats for LA's Artful-Dodgers in a twi-night doubleheader at mile-high altitude. To his further frustration, his wife and newborn namesake were at home, hundreds of miles away. Lonely and sleepless, Peter found more than the simple diversion he sought by turning on the TV. The spectacle of Willy–an elegant, graceful, and intensely aggressive powerhouse of a pitcher–sparked the glimmer of an idea that would lay dormant in Peter's mind until he had the opportunity to act on it six years later.

Chapter 1

She turned up the volume on the stereo so that the music would follow her vacuuming throughout the house. She kicked her leg high in the air as she swung the vacuum's power-head around the living room and bent backwards as she ran the head through the space between the bottom of the couch and the deep pile of the carpet. She barely heard the phone ringing over the rhythm of the music and the drone of the vacuum cleaner. Only the discordant note of the bell tone signaled its presence against the wall of sound surrounding her. She tapped the foot-switch with her toe, scooped the receiver off its cradle, spun herself around, and flopped down on the couch with one leg slung over the edge of the armrest.

"Willy?" came a voice.

"Yeah!"

"It's Peter . . . Peter Jones," the voice said.

She sang, "The MVP from LA!"

"Not anymore!" he laughed. "Don't you read the sports pages, girl? They traded me to Buffalo."

"Buffalo! Isn't that the last stop in the major leagues?" she scoffed.

"It used to be," said Peter with a trace of laughter in his voice. "They get paid on Thursdays, just like LA. That's what counts. The front office knows I want to manage someday, so they sent me to Florida to work with our Instructional League team in Orlando. The Wolves have some good young players in their system. The kids are mostly first-year minor leaguers, but a couple of them can play in the bigs now, I think."

"I want you to come and see me while you're down here," said Willy.

"That's why I called. I have some free time this afternoon."

"Oh, uh, okay," she stammered nervously, caught off guard. "But I gotta work. I coach the girls' track team at the high school. We have a one-hour practice at three. Visit me there."

"See you then," said Peter, after Willy gave him directions to Old Saint Petersburg Bay High School.

Willy Mae Beal's days were filled by a rigorous regimen of running, aerobics, meditation, yoga, and workouts with "my kids" at school. Her nights were filled by her second love, music, either with her fingers at the piano or through the headphones of her pocket-sized music player. She practiced Zen and vegetarianism, attended an occasional dance class, and threw a hundred pitches with a baseball in her mother's backyard for at least an hour a day–every day. For Willy, and millions of other baseball junkies, it wasn't just the best game in the world, it was the *only* game.

Willy's passion for the game was, quite literally, in her blood. Her grandfather, Reuben Henry, had been a professional baseball player for three decades. Papp, as Willy called him, spent the better part of his life playing ball and the latter part teaching it, along with its secrets and its stories, to his granddaughter, thereby uniting his life's work with the love of his life. Rube Henry died two years ago, but a piece of his soul would live on whenever Willy Beal wrapped her fingers around the seams of a baseball.

Willy was anxious to get to the field and put her squad through its workout so that she could enjoy her visit with Peter Jones, an old family friend with parallel roots planted deeply in the Grand Old Game's subculture. Leaving her vacuuming undone, Willy pulled back her hair with a sweatband, put on her holey sneakers, strapped on her carryall bag, clipped her Running Mate to her back pocket, plugged the music into her ears, and set out on the five-mile run to work.

At the schoolyard, the sprinters had sprinted and the hurdlers had hurdled by the time Peter arrived. When Willy spotted him across the field, walking past the soccer team's scrimmage, she caught his eye with a wave.

"C'mon y'all," Willy called out to her charges while clapping her hands. "Let's take a lap and knock off early." She greeted Peter with a sweet smile and a taunting laugh. "I bet you got lost."

"No way! I was watching the hoofers over there," he said with a backward jerk of his thumb.

"Good, 'cause nobody else does. This is pigskin and hoop country. Folks don't even know we have a soccer team."

Peter was wearing dress slacks, a sport coat, highly polished shoes, and a white shirt open at the neck. His conservative attire belied the broad chest and thick limbs of a professional athlete.

"How're you doing, Peter?"

"Good," Peter said cheerily. "Working with the Instructional League was a lot of fun. Next, they're sending me to Santo Domingo to take in a few winter league games. Remember old Tito Melendez?"

"Hasn't he retired yet?"

"I guess this is a comeback—one more time again. They say he's learned to throw a split-fingered fastball. I'll be scouting him for the Wolves. We might sign him if he looks good."

Willy, smiling extravagantly since Peter arrived, took hold of his arm and said, "Let's walk and talk."

"Where're we going?" he asked as he complied, letting her lead him along.

"The baseball field's over on the other side of the building. Where else?"

"I'll feel right at home," said Peter. He was just a bit uncomfortable, not at walking arm in arm with Willy, but at the clusters of young, fresh-faced women in tee-shirts and shorts who were milling around the track and gawking at them.

"Thanks for coming to the funeral when my grandfather passed," Willy said in a softened voice.

"Well, he played ball with my daddy, and they were friends. That's important. He wanted to come himself, but it's like he got old real fast after my mother died."

"They'd always be talking about the old days," declared Willy, shaking her head with a melancholy smile. She tilted her head skyward with a nostalgic look in her dazzling brown eyes. "Barnstorming with Dizzy Dean and Satchel Paige, playing in Mexico with Sal Maglie and Dolph Luque after the war, playing all summer long and going to southern California to play in the winter."

"And Cuba," added Peter.

"They played with Luis Tiant's daddy."

"And Puerto Rico . . ."

"They played with Orlando Cepeda's daddy."

"And Venezuela . . ."

"They played with Luis Aparicio's daddy. Did your father ever tell you about the year they played on the Dominican dictator's team?"

"Yeah! What was his name—Battista?"

"No, he was the one in Cuba who came to all the ballgames. It was Trujillo."

"Yeah, that's it Trujillo," Peter laughed. "He not only owned the whole country, he had to own the best team himself."

"Papp said they had troops all around the stadium for the championship game and the guys were scared they'd get shot if they lost," Willy said.

"Not much chance of that with Satch, Josh Gibson, and Cool Papa Bell all on the same team," Peter said.

Willy was clinging to Peter's arm, tugging it with a convulsive laugh as they shared bits and pieces of memory. She said, "Papp and Amos remembered every game they played and every player they knew, it seems."

"Yeah," agreed Peter, "and I think *you* remember every story they ever told."

"Uh-huh," Willy sang joyfully. "Those were my bedtime stories."

Peter changed the subject, or, at least, its focus. "I have a two-year contract from the Wolves, with an option for a third. I think I can play three more years. I'd like to play five, but as good as the people in Buffalo are, they're not going to keep me around if I can't hit better than .239 like this past year. This is my third team. I don't want to move again if I can help it. I've seen guys on the way down who turned into hired guns—have bat, will travel! I can't do that."

"Will you be a designated hitter in Buffalo?" Willy asked.

Peter shook his head. "I met Nick Dolan, the manager. He said it'd be up to me to quit playing right field. He said, 'You still have the great arm.' Hell, it's my legs that hurt, not my arm, but I'll keep shagging flies as long as I can."

Peter Jones was at a transition in his life and his career. He was closing in on the age of forty, a shuddering realization for many an aging athlete, playing instead of working for a living.

"I *know* I can manage a team in the bigs," he said, as if expecting an argument. "But I have to prove it. There's *still* an old-boy network. It's just not the same old boys! I look at my brother, James, and it just makes me mad. He's been managing in the Tex-Mex League for five seasons and never finished lower than second with one of his teams." Peter was now waving his arms in agitation. "And he can't get any job in the bigs—except as a batting instructor."

Willy, however, knew that James "Jimmy Mack" Jones was different from his younger brother. Peter was a "name" player, and if anything would prevent him from becoming a big league field pilot, it was the stigma of stardom. Players of that level are often presumed to have difficulty tolerating the lesser skills of the ordinary athlete.

"That's why I'm heading down to Venezuela next. I landed a job as skipper of a winter league team."

"You're kiddin' me!" Willy cried.

"James had a team down there last year," continued Peter, "and he'll be back again. He and I will have our own little friendly family feud going on."

Then said Willy, smilingly, but somberly, "What goes around comes around. You're retracing your daddy's footsteps."

"In a way, I suppose so."

Chapter 2

Willy and Peter reached the baseball field and went to the metallic bleachers behind the green chain-link backstop.

"Whatever happened to wood?" Peter mused.

"Ha! Whatever happened to bleachers? The grandstand seats in the majors aren't real bleachers anymore."

Willy playfully walked on her toes over the benchlike seats with her arms outstretched. Peter looked over at a group of half a dozen kids, male and female, several yards away. He recognized two of them as Willy's tracksters. "They're following us!" Peter exclaimed.

"They're checking you out, Peter," responded Willy, as she sat herself down. "Wondering who you are and what you're talking to me for."

Willy sat with her long legs dangling onto the next row of seats, propping herself up with her arms, hands palms down, and her head thrown back leisurely. Peter studied this quieter, calmer Willy. After a few minutes he leaned back on the bleachers, mimicking her posture, and closed his eyes.

Willy startled Peter by suddenly grabbing and pulling his arm. "C'mon! Let's have some fun."

"What? Here?" protested Peter. "I'm kind of overdressed. Wouldn't you say?"

Without further debate, Willy vaulted to her feet and called out, "Jennifer!" to one of the youngsters milling about nearby. One of the young women that Peter had noticed before came running toward them, setting her sun-bleached blonde hair swirling around her head and shoulders.

"Yes, Coach Beal?" she asked with eagerness.

"You know where they keep the baseball equipment?" Willy pulled a ring full of tinkling keys from her shorts' pocket. Jennifer nodded as she cupped her hands to catch Willy's toss of the keys. Willy flashed a pleased-with-herself grin and said to Peter, "She'll be back in a sec."

"You're a kick, Willy," he laughed.

"How's Darlene?" Willy asked, evidently making small talk to pass the time.

"It's Charlene!" corrected Peter.

"How's *Char*-lene?"

"She's fine," said Peter, "but she's getting tired of being married to a ballplayer, you know. She's not tired of me, I don't think. It's the life. It's not really normal; like how she, not me, taught Peter Junior how to swing a baseball bat. I came home from a road trip . . . she's left-handed, so she's got him batting that way, even though he's a righty. I couldn't believe it, but I couldn't change him around either. That's how he learned." He paused briefly before saying, "Charlene just got used to me being home for four or five months between seasons. Now, I'm going off to do winter ball in South America, and I'm talking about staying in the game and being a manager for the next twenty years."

"What does she do?" Willy wondered.

"She's a psychotherapist—drug abuse, alcohol abuse, sexual

abuse. She counsels kids, adults, families, and groups. There's a lot of abuse out there. It's tough work, but Char's pretty tough, too. She loves her work. She's passionate about it."

"Smart lady, huh?"

"Yeah," Peter said proudly. "She sure is."

"Will you move to Buffalo?" Willy asked.

Peter nodded. "It makes sense. Char can do what she does anywhere and we made a mistake by not living in LA. We stayed in Arizona."

This time Willy changed the subject. "Our varsity softball team was pretty good last spring," she said. "We played tournaments on weekends in the fall and indoors in the winter. We're looking to send all nine starters to college on scholarships. For some of these girls, this sport is a one-way ticket out. Like Jennifer . . . "

"Which one is she?"

"The cute girl with the big hair," said Willy, gesturing toward the well-muscled and attractive teenager, who at that moment was emerging from a doorway, sweating and struggling to carry two canvas equipment bags—one over each shoulder. Her friends were razzing her from afar.

"They're *all* cute . . . because they're young!" Peter laughed as Willy rose to take him to the baseball diamond.

"She's a three-sport athlete," replied Willy. "She's strong and she works out, but she loves her pizza and potato chips and ice cream and soda pop. I have to frisk her for cigarettes, too!"

"You're hard, Willy," teased Peter. Then, he asked, "What about you? Do you play much these days?"

She nodded, "Uh-huh!" as she skipped off the lowest row of benches and skidded her sneakers into the dirt. "I played slow-pitch and fast-pitch with two different softball teams.

My fast-pitch team went to the national tournament in Minot, North Dakota last August. There were some incredible–I mean, *incredible*–pitchers there. At least in fast-pitch you can do something with the ball. Girls like Jenny Finch, Cat Osterman, and Lisa Fernandez can throw a drop, a rise, and a change-up as well as a windmill fastball. In slow-pitch softball, you have to put the ball over the plate with an arc that's at least above the batter's shoulders. That's more like pitching horseshoes than baseball, but I came up with kind of a slider-curve, sort of an Eephus pitch, like Rip Sewell and Spaceman Bill Lee used to throw."

Willy demonstrated her finger grip on an invisible, imaginary ball and didn't see the incredulous look on Peter's face. *How can she throw a "slurve" underhand with a twelve-inch softball?*

Willy quickened her steps toward Jennifer, who had lain down the bags of balls, bats, mitts, and sundry hardball hardware at the edge of the backstop. "Thanks, Jennifer," said Willy. "We're gonna play some pitch-and-hit."

"Can I catch?" asked the cute girl with big hair.

"Sure, but just roll the balls to the backstop and fetch them later. We don't want to stop after each pitch, waiting for you to toss the ball back."

Peter Jones picked up and discarded several bats before grabbing a lightweight aluminum one. Willy was already standing on the mound with several balls cradled in her arms and a fielder's glove dangling from her pinky.

"Don't you dare use that tinny bat. . . "

"Are you serious? Never!" declared one of the real men who use real wood. He found a piece of timber to his liking, rolled up his shirtsleeves, and stepped to the plate. He called out to Willy, "Hey, does this sort of remind you of a scene from a movie?"

"Yeah!" answered Willy. "Roy Hobbs and The Whammer!"

"You know, the movie ended with *The Natural* hitting a homer, but in the book by Malamud he struck out," said Peter, the college English major, kicking his toes and then his heels into the dirt before stepping back to smooth it all over again with the sole of his left shoe.

"That's more realistic," said Willy. "Like Joannie Joyce against Ted Williams and Hank Aaron!"

"Oh, now, that wasn't a fair test. She struck them both out with a softball," protested Peter.

"But Hammerin' Hank started out as a softball player," countered Willy.

Peter smiled as if to concede the point. Willy was standing at the mound, turned sideways with the ball concealed in her gloved left hand. She tucked her right hand into the pocket of the glove and drew both hands in toward her waist, ready to pitch from the "stretch" position.

"Do you need to warm up?" Peter inquired.

"No, I throw for an hour every day before work."

"Yeah?" He narrowed his eyes quizzically, swinging his bat lazily to and fro. "Why?"

"Good exercise!"

"Whatever you say!"

Willy threw easily and Peter swung half-heartedly at one, two, three, four pitches. "Wanna see my slider? . . . Wanna see me throw it sidearm? . . . Now, three-quarters overhand—I call that the buggywhip," Willy sang happily. She threw one low-and-away slider. He flicked at it. She threw another and he tipped it into the dirt.

"Not half bad!" he said to her.

"Now I'm coming through the back door!" she yelled and

threw a sidearm slider that sped toward his midsection before slicing down and away at his knees over the inside corner of the plate. He didn't swing.

"Time to get serious, now!" he decreed.

Willy stood at the pitcher's rubber, smiling slightly. Peter showed not a hint of a smile. Willy thought about how sportswriters and sportscasters would say Peter Jones, with his broad back and thick arms, was built more like a football linebacker than a baseball player. Willy realized she was standing sixty feet, six inches away from someone who had hit more than 500 big league home runs. She felt a surge of adrenalin flow through her body with a rush more intense than anything she had experienced since her failed tryout with Olympic Team USA five years ago. She was woozy and light-headed as she went into her pitching motion with her arms and legs trembling and then she reared back her right arm, snarled, and kicked her left leg toward the sky to unleash Papp's heater, the old-fashioned, down-home fastball that Willy's grandfather taught her to throw when she was nine years old.

Willy's eyes followed the ball toward the plate as Peter strode into the pitch to swing and she watched his knees buckle as his bat whipped under it. He stumbled backward a few steps, then put one hand on his hip and balanced himself on the bat as if it were a cane.

"What the hell was that?" shouted the former MVP from LA.

"Just my fastball," answered Willy with a playfully coquettish wink.

That was not Randy Johnson or Pedro Martinez standing out there, dressed in an orange headband and matching scrunchie, faded cut-offs, white tee shirt, and knee socks, thought Peter. Yet the way that fastball jumped about two feet in front of the plate, she might as well be any of the great ones he had faced. If thrown properly, a fastball indeed rises, maybe only half an inch during its journey from the mound to home plate, but it does rise. Willy hadn't brought the pitch to Peter with hundred-mile-an-hour velocity, but it was probably close to ninety. Anyway, as the truism goes, "It's not the speed, it's the movement." Whether her "action" on the ball was real or an optical illusion made little difference to Peter. Unless it was a fluke, he was convinced that he couldn't hit her pitching.

Willy was holding the ball, ready to pitch again. Jennifer was now standing, not crouching, behind the batter's box, making no pretense of trying to catch the ball and just fetching each pitch after it hit the backstop.

"Come on with it!" Peter called. Willy nodded wordlessly. This time she came around sidearm, slightly offspeed, but with the same lively movement ahead of Peter's too early swing.

"Cut that stuff out!" he shouted angrily. "No more sidearm, sliders, buggywhips, all that stuff! Just bring me that straight-ahead fastball, overhand!"

"You got it!" said Willy, and she fired the heater knee-high on the inside corner, belt-high on the outside corner, belt-high on the inside corner, and knee-high on the outside corner. She had perfect command of the strike zone, and Peter had managed to foul off only two of the four pitches thrown.

Next, she laid one chest-high over the middle of the plate and he rippled at it once more. "Sonofa . . . !" She taunted him with a "meatball" and beat him.

Several more high schoolers joined those following Peter

and Willy around the schoolyard to watch the batter-pitcher duel unfolding. "Hey, ain't he somebody?" said one of the members of the boys' track team.

"Check it out, my man. She's eatin' him up. The dude can't hit nothin'!"

Peter stepped backward, further from the mound and closer to the plate, deeper in the unmarked batter's box. His front foot rested on the black strip of rubber outlining the dish and he began to kick away swirls of dirt with the heel of his back foot.

Whiz! Plunk! "Sorry!" said Willy, as Peter made a show of rubbing the spot on his rib cage where the ball struck. "But don't be digging in like that against me anymore!"

"Are you trying to kill me or what?" he said sharply.

"Of course not," she chirped, taking a few steps toward him. "If I was trying to kill you, I'd have thrown shoulder high, behind your back, so you'd duck your head right into it." Willy raised her long, elegant forefinger to point between her eyes and smiled.

"Did ol' Rube teach you that?" Peter asked irritably.

"Papp showed me how, but he told me don't ever do it."

Peter Jones rocked, shifting his weight from front foot to back, left foot to right, and twirled his bat in tight, concentric circles. The woman standing atop the pitcher's mound showed neither impatience nor hurry as she waited for his body to tense and stiffen for the next pitch. Willy's next pitch was a change-up that stayed flat and sailed inward, instead of rising. Peter twisted his wrists and made contact, pulling the ball toward first base. His smile at having broken the ice by putting the wood to the ball was answered by three consecutive tight pitches at his fists, his chin, and his nose. Peter Jones felt a familiar twinge of fear as the woman with the pretty brown eyes bit her lower lip, shrieked, and hurled yet another fastball a few inches from his head. The fear was nothing new. It would come—the hollowness in his stomach would swell to nausea, then set his pulse racing and his breath quickening until he wanted to cry out—then he would swallow and it would go away. Yet he only experienced such fear in fan-filled stadia—never in a schoolyard, never while facing an amateur pitcher.

Willy drew her left hand downward to meet her other hand, which held the ball and came out from behind her back. She swiveled on her right heel, drew up her left leg, kicked outward, and twisted around a semicircular arc as her right arm cocked, straightened, and delivered the bullet-like white pill from her dancing fingers. This time, the pitch thrown overhand seemed to spin on its side, signaling a slider. "She's playing with me," thought Peter. "I'll tag it!" He stepped into the pitch and swung, but it didn't break. Rather, it rose over his slicing bat. "A darn cutter!" he hissed bitterly, scaring Jennifer, the catcher of the day.

Of the next twenty pitches that Willy threw, Peter hit five grounders, six foul balls, and one line drive that came back at Willy like a flash of light in front of her eyes. She skinned her knees, hitting the ground, as the ball hummed past her ear.

"Now you're trying to kill *me*!"

"Sorry," mocked Peter Jones.

He checked his swing on the next pitch, a high and outside "heater" that came to the plate with as much movement and velocity as the first one Willy threw, and he smashed the four pitches that followed for line drives to Willy's left and right. The crowd of teenagers surrounding them clapped and cheered for the assistant track coach, who took home a salary of $500 a month, to keep scorching the visiting celebrity whose pro contract paid millions a year. The last pitch of the schoolyard duel was another off-speed fastball that trailed in, instead of rising, and Peter stroked it over second base and into center field.

The kids hooted, but then applauded in appreciation for the show, as Peter shouted, "That's it! Done!" and slammed his bat onto the ground. He wore a smile as he approached Willy, but the rage in her eyes didn't bode well for an invitation to dinner.

"You had to beat me, didn't you?" she spat bitterly. "Can't let a woman strike you out, right?" Her voice cracked and she winced.

Peter met her outburst with a restrained laugh. "Are you serious?" he quipped, trying to make eye contact, but she cast her gaze to her feet. Peter placed a hand on each of her shoulders and said, "Listen to me, Willy." She looked up without raising her head. "Yeah, I hit you . . . after you made me look like a chump twenty or thirty times! I'm a professional. I've been hitting baseballs for a living for fifteen years."

She wrinkled her nose, flashed a false toothy smile, and whispered, "Yeah, so what?"

"Hey, let me tell you something," he said. "I face three thousand live pitches in a hundred and sixty-two real games every season. I swing at hundreds more in batting practice each day, each week, all year long." He paused as she wiggled her shoulders to release his hold. Instead of letting go, Peter gave Willy a gentle shake. "And what you were throwing was as good as anything I've seen in the bigs. Do you understand what I'm saying to you?"

Willy tilted her head, slightly curling her lips to say, "You think I'm good, huh?"

"You're good, all right," Peter chuckled. *So good it's downright scary*, he thought in silence.

Peter was tired, sweaty, and dirty, but Willy was refreshed with exhilaration. She raised her arms to remove her damp orange headband, wrapped the scrunchie around her fingers, gave her head a shake, and flipped her hair to the front, covering the right side of her face.

"Did you ever think about . . ." Peter began with high seriousness.

"Think about what?" she replied, stroking and fingering her hair before pulling the headband on her forehead once again.

"A tryout," he pronounced.

"I've been wanting to go to a fantasy camp, but it costs three or four thousand dollars. Maybe next year . . . "

"I'm not talking about that!" Peter said with a note of anger surfacing in his voice. "You don't need to be any good to play around with a bunch of out-of-shape old men."

"This isn't Papp and Amos's days, Peter," Willy said soberly. "Teams don't hold tryout camps anymore. Scouts don't beat the bushes for raw talent out in the sticks anymore. They all scout the same high school and college kids, read the same scouting reports, and draft from the same list of prospects. Isn't that true?"

"Did you ever ask anybody for a tryout?" Peter was being insistent.

"Oh, yeah?" she said defiantly, bobbing on her toes, accentuating her superior height. "How many women are going with you to spring training with the Wolves?"

"Maybe you could be the first," he said cheerfully.

"No, sir!" she said with a lecturing point of her finger. "Long before *A League of Their Own*, there were teams like the

Bloomer Girls and the Ranger Girls, players like Maude Nelson, Lizzie Murphy, Edith Houghton, Toni Stone, and Jackie Mitchell–a southpaw, only seventeen years old, who whiffed number three and number four in pinstripes, back to back." *Snap, snap, snap!* went Willy's fingers. "And Ila Borders pitched for an independent league team in the '90s."

"So, why not Willy?" he asked.

"We all have dreams, Peter," she said in reply. "And then we grow up. You . . . you're one of the chosen ones."

"Chosen one? Ha! You cut my balls off with that slider of yours."

"Shush!" said Willy in a playful rebuke. "None of that nasty talk! There are children here."

"Children, you say?" Peter took a glance over his shoulder at Jennifer and Tanya, both of whom had tried to catch his eye with their swaying hips and fluttering lashes.

Willy tried to push her elbow into his stomach. "I'll tell Darlene on you–you old married man!"

"It's *Char*-lene." Peter followed Willy into the school building by way of a side door.

"If we go in through the locker room, the girls will attack you. It's no-man's land. Get it?"

"I got it," he chuckled, as they walked in the direction of an opened office door.

Willy asked Peter, "You wanna run over to the other locker room and hop in the shower?"

He shrugged and held out his open palms. "I have nothing to change into. Why bother?"

"The word's gonna get around that you're here. If the principal's still in the building, he'll be down to kiss your butt."

He laughed, taking a seat on the desk's edge. "You're a

kick, Willy! Should I be polite when I bend over. Are they treating you right?"

"Yeah, they're okay. I coach the jay-vee track and softball teams, and I run an aerobic exercise class for the football team. I wanted to teach a health and nutrition class, too, but. . ."

"Coach Beal, can I use the phone?" A tall young woman appeared in the doorway, tapping her fingers on the molding and rhythmically chewing a piece of gum.

"What happened to your cell, Tanya?" Willy inquired suspiciously.

"It died," Tanya replied. Willy, unsmiling, gestured toward the telephone on the desk. Tanya blew a pink bubble, popped it, and slinked past Peter, with whom she exchanged a smile. Willy rolled her eyes in disapproval. Tanya's athletic physique slumped into poor posture as she began long, slow dialing. "Moms? Yeah! I been at practice . . . Of course, I'm sure . . . No, I'm goin' out after school . . . Nowhere! . . . Nothin'! . . . Huh? I changed the baby before I come to school . . . Did too! Listen, Moms, I gotta go . . . " The receiver went *slam!* onto its cradle and Tanya sauntered from the room.

Willy shook her head. "Bless you, Tanya. You'll get by. The whole world turns around her, day after day, and she doesn't give it a thought. Babies having babies! She hands it to her mother and goes on back to school."

"The way it is today," said Peter, "a kid getting pregnant is hardly the worst thing that can happen. Drugs, AIDS, STDs, gangs, violence . . . and video games!"

"She's one of those girls whose body matured in middle school, but the rest of her never caught up," said Willy, pointing to her temple. Peter Jones just smiled without comment. Willy continued, "She's a good athlete. She comes

Willy's Ballgame

from a good home–good people! Her parents do everything for her. They're raising her baby while she's out partying all night long . . . Then there's Jennifer. Her family's all screwed up, let me tell you! She should be all messed up, but she's not. She's an angel compared to Tanya."

After a moment, Peter said, "You really care about them, don't you?"

Willy nodded with a smile. "Yeah, I do," she said.

"You're quite a lady, Willy Beal."

She said, "Thank you," in a barely audible whisper. Then she smiled. "Coming to dinner? Mama would love to see you."

"Definitely!"

"Let me call her, real quick," she said. Peter noticed how she clicked off seven digits, using all five lightning-fast fingers, in no more than two seconds. On the phone with her mother, Alma, Willy said, "I made up some ratatouille. It's in the freezer. You just zap it in the microwave and make a salad . . . Mama! No, not fried chicken! Yeah! Uh-huh! Okay, Mama . . . love you, too. Bye!"

Said Peter, "I'm riding around in a rental car."

"I'll give you directions. Our house is only about five miles away. I'll meet you there in twenty minutes."

"Why don't I follow you in your car?" he asked.

Willy smiled. "Willy runs."

When Peter drove his rented subcompact down the street of small, tightly packed, single-family homes where Willy and Alma lived, he checked the digital clock on the dashboard. Twenty-five minutes had elapsed, and he found Willy seated triumphantly on her mother's doorstep.

"Have you ever thought about running marathons?" he asked, quite impressed with her time.

"Well, seriously, yeah," said Willy as she unbent her superb legs to stand. "But when I got to the point where I could go five miles, then ten miles, and then twenty-six miles without hitting the wall of pain, I started to ask myself, 'Where am I going anyway?' I got bored."

Peter, accustomed to dashing a mere ninety feet to first base, just shook his head and laughed.

Alma Henry Beal met Willy and Peter at the door, exclaiming, "What in the world have you two been doing?" Alma pursed her lips and waved her hands at the two sweaty bodies that flanked her.

"We played some ball in the schoolyard," Willy said matter-of-factly. She leaned against Peter's shoulder and wrinkled her nose. "Of course, I live here. So, I can go shower and change before dinner. You can't, ha!" With that, Willy wagged her tongue at him and scampered upstairs.

"I have the most beautiful daughter a mother could ask for," Alma said to Peter, but her hands and eyes turned skyward as if to invoke heavenly wisdom. "She's twenty-seven years old and still a child; she's living at home . . . not married . . . and forever playing boys' games!" Then Alma's face burst into a smile as radiant as her daughter's and she greeted Peter with a warm embrace. At the dinner table, Alma told Peter, "Willy Mae used to sing in church every Sunday and we used to say grace before the evening meal . . . until she became a *Buddhist!*" Willy slowly twirled her fork amidst the rice and vegetables on her plate without casting an eye on her mother, who continued, "We disagree over what to say, how to say it, and apparently *whom* to say it to!"

"Mama, please!" Willy whined as she let her fork drop with a clang.

"Willie Davis and Dave Henderson were Buddhists," said

Peter, trying to be conciliatory.

"I'm not a Buddhist!" Willy hissed petulantly.

"Willy Mae doesn't eat meat," Alma said. "Now, I don't disagree with that at all."

"Char's gotten me to cut way back on . . . " Peter started to speak before realizing that his mouth was better off shut as Alma lectured.

"There's not a thing wrong with chicken or fish or red meat in moderation, but Willy Mae won't hear of it. I just don't know how she gets enough iron or protein because she won't take a supplement. She will not ingest a pill!"

"Mama, why're you getting on my case in front of company?" Willy implored, but she didn't shout.

"Amos and Louise Jones's son is not company!" Alma declared. "Why, Amos and your grandfather worked together longer than Papp was married to my mother." Reaching her hand to pat his, Alma said softly, "Peter's practically family." With Willy's attention momentarily diverted, Alma silently mouthed the words, "She *is* a Buddhist," and Peter smiled with a nod.

Later, Willy and Peter went outside to chat on the back porch. There was a cool evening breeze and the sounds of people laughing and an infant crying came from a neighbor's opened window. Willy sat upon the porch rail with knees drawn up under her chin and arms folded around her legs, actually hugging herself, Peter observed.

"Alma's a nice lady," Peter said fondly. "Does she have a boyfriend?"

"Yeah, my mama has a boyfriend," answered Willy. "Only a respectable, church-going gentleman, of course."

"She's a nurse, isn't she?"

"Nurse practitioner, if you please," said Willy with a hint

of pride in her voice.

"Do you think she'll get married again someday?" Peter wondered. "She's still young."

"No," Willy said with certainty. "It wasn't all that good with my father, Eddy."

"Did he drink?" Peter surprised Willy with his straightforwardness.

"No . . . I mean, yeah . . . " Willy sighed loudly. "He didn't treat us bad. He just wasn't there." She looked out into the night and seemed to hug herself more tightly. "He wasn't evil. He just died young."

"They say that's how it goes with marriages. People that have had a good one will do it again," Peter observed. Without waiting for her to say anything more, Peter nudged Willy's side with his forefinger and climbed onto the railing next to her. "Listen, Willy, I have to ask you something," Peter said somewhat ominously. "I've had an idea for a while now and what happened out on that ballfield just nailed it."

"It sounds serious," Willy said wistfully. "Well, spit it out, Peter Jones."

"The team I'll be managing in Venezuela has given me pretty much a free hand to bring aboard any players I want. Things are a little looser in winter ball. I'm bringing four guys from the Wolves organization to play for me down there." He paused and looked Willy squarely in the eye to say, "Come with us."

"Don't play with me!" she said in a hushed, hoarse whisper.

"I'm serious, Willy. The winter league season's from November 'til the first week of February. We play thirty games. The pay is peanuts. It barely covers living expenses . . . " He stopped talking as Willy stepped down from the railing and began to pace, shaking her head.

"I don't know. I'll have to quit my job and . . . "

"You call that a job?" he said provocatively.

"Don't you dare diss me like that!" she said, more hurt than angry. She rubbed her still-crossed arms as if the air had turned cold.

"I'm not dissing you, Willy." Peter reached for her hand and she let him hold it. "Maybe I'm over the hill, but anybody who can hang me out to dry like you did today . . . You owe it to yourself to give it a shot." Then, demonstratively pointing at her, he said, "Don't try to tell me you never thought about it!"

With a jerk of her head that dropped a wisp of hair across her face, Willy said, "Of course, I've thought about it. Every blessed day of my life!" Her voice quivered and she took a deep breath.

"Then go for it, girl," Peter said gently. "There's nothing keeping you here."

Willy Mae Beal didn't answer but said, "Let's get on back inside. We're being rude to Mama."

With a nod, Peter said, "I'll call you in a couple of weeks. Think it over."

Chapter 3

Willy always did her throwing with a bucket or bag full of balls so that she could toss ten or twenty pitches at the bull's-eye in the center of a padded backstop without the need to chase after each one. Whenever she bought some new baseballs, she would sit on the grass and place them around her, hold each one, and twirl it around her fingers before she was ready to throw it.

Even when she was seriously competing in softball as a teenager, Willy did five minutes of throwing underhand, then five minutes overhand, followed by ten or twenty minutes with a hardball, overhead and underhand. Before Papp died, ever since she was too young to remember, she played ball in Alma's backyard with him. They played one-on-one, pitching, hitting, and fielding. As she grew up and he grew older, their games became slower, more tutorial. "Always throw the same pitch the same way out of your hand. A fastball's a fastball if it's sidearm, overhand, or crackin' the buggywhip. Ya got three ways to throw it to fool the batter, but don't fool your own self. It's the same heater." Their games were a grandfather and granddaughter bonding, visitations on common ground, a kind of ritual of love. The afternoons of Willy's childhood consisted of arriving home from school, doing an hour or two of homework, half an hour of scales and five-finger exercises at the piano, and waiting for Papp to say, "That's enough for today, li'l gal. Let's go play some ball."

After Willy returned home from college, after failing to make the grade with Team USA and having no other teams to play with or try out for, she and Papp resumed their backyard games, a diversion for them both. On one such afternoon, not long before his passing, Papp wrapped his arms around Willy. She returned his hug, noticing how tired and sad he suddenly looked.

"What's the matter, Papp?"

"Nothin'," he said. "I was just thinkin', if things was different, ya'd be pitchin' in the big time by now."

"You think so?"

"I surely do." Rube Henry never told his adoring granddaughter he wished she had been born a male, but she always knew he did.

Two weeks had passed since she last saw Peter Jones. October turned into November, and Willy doubted that she would hear from him. Men always promised things they couldn't deliver, saying they wanted to call, but never picking up the phone. When Peter and Willy met again one day, he might tell her, "I forgot to call," characteristically preferring the appearance of imbecility to honesty—"I changed my mind about it"—or weakness—"I couldn't pull it off." A winter season of ball playing in Venezuela with living and breathing big leaguers seemed like just another unrealized dream. However, once the dream was dangled in front of her, Willy was tantalized by the prospect. Her real life, which itself wasn't at all what she had planned, was now something she no longer wanted.

Willy reclined on her bed to meditate, humming softly, her bedroom full of fragrant incense, when the ring of her cell phone cracked through her thoughts. She opened her eyes at the first ring. She jumped from the bed to answer after the second ring.

"Yeah!"

"Hey, Willy, it's Peter. Are you ready to go?"

Willy wanted to cry out for joy. She cleared her throat to speak, afraid that she might sob. "I almost gave up on you."

"Listen," said Peter. "I'm really sorry for not getting back to you sooner. I got hung up going back and forth from Tucson to Buffalo looking for a house for us, but I couldn't find anything . . . "

"They don't have houses for sale in Buffalo, New York?" she kidded.

Peter laughed through the long-distance fibers. "Nothing I looked at was quite right. You know what I mean? Charlene's going to have to find something by herself while I'm away."

"You play while she works, right?" Willy mused.

"Anyway," Peter went on, "the season's starting in three days, so . . . "

"You're kiddin' me, Peter Jones!" she shouted. "How do you expect me to turn my life upside down and get my butt to South America in three days?"

"Calm down, Willy. Stop yelling at me," he chortled. "Let me give you my credit card number so you can catch a plane out of Tampa tomorrow. Check online and see what you can get."

"Tomorrow," she grumbled. "Shots, passport, money!"

"I'm taking a late flight tonight. I'll meet you at the airport in Caracas. Text me your flight number once you have it.

James and I are renting a villa on Lake Maracaibo. Can you believe it? A villa! There's lots of room, so you and the other guys from the States can move in with us."

"Just us guys, huh? Sounds like fun!" She snorted a laugh. "Peter? Thank you."

"Don't thank me," he said. "You've got a thirty-game season to show the world what you can do. Let's just go do it."

First thing the next morning Willy called the school district's athletic director to tell him she would be taking three months off and he promptly fired her. "That was easy," she said to herself. More difficult was that she didn't have time to say goodbye to her kids, especially Jennifer and troublesome Tanya. Willy intended to send them postcards, but forgot to jot down their home addresses before departing. She packed two backpacks full of necessities: underwear, white socks, batteries for her Running Mate and dozens of CDs, a pile of books, and a pocket-sized Spanish-English dictionary left over from college, her fancy "going-out" shoes, and an unopened package of pantyhose purchased more than a year ago should anything of a social nature develop. *Oops! You almost forgot your baseball glove, Willy.*

Alma was naturally confused, since Willy hadn't hinted at the possibility of playing for Peter's team in Venezuela. *Surprise!* Her daughter was going away, leaving the country, in fact, with less than a day's notice. The emotional energy was high as Alma watched Willy scavenge the bathroom medicine chest for toiletries.

"Don't forget a toothbrush, for goodness sake!"

"I won't, Mama!" Willy snapped curtly.

"And tampons! Can you even get them in that country?"

"Okay, Mama," Willy whispered through grinding teeth.

"I just don't understand you, Willy Mae." Alma's anger brewed. "You have the voice of an angel." Her anger simmered. "You hear a melody once and you can play it on the piano." Her anger boiled.

"Mama don't!"

"But you gave up studying music to become an athlete."

"Mama, please."

"You broke my heart!" Alma cried.

"I'll dream my own dreams, thank you."

"You didn't get your college degree. You don't have a career. You turned your back on the church. You say you want a family, but you don't have a husband or even a boyfriend . . ."

"Yo, woman, go mate!" Willy mocked.

"Watch your mouth with me," Alma said sternly through her tears.

"I'm sorry, Mama." Willy, herself on the verge of crying, said, "Don't you understand I have to do this?"

"Your grandfather did this to you," Alma accused.

"Papp was *your* father," said Willy, taken aback.

"That's right," said Rube's daughter. "He said he never saw me grow up. So, he was going to make sure he stuck around for you."

"He . . . I mean, the two of you . . . raised me," said Rube's granddaughter. "And didn't we need him to be there for us?"

Alma nodded her agreement but then said, "And while I was working two jobs, day and night, to pay for dance and piano lessons, he'd have you out in the yard throwing a baseball. He brought you into *his* world."

Willy gazed at her mother diagonally through the bathroom commode mirror. "You know something, Mama? Feels like we're back in my teens again, when we couldn't share the same space for more than ten minutes before we locked horns."

Alma laughed and blinked, a tear falling from her lashes. She said, "It was all runaway hormones, shuttling from one activity to another, and never enough time to do your homework." Now Willy laughed and stroked her mother's shoulder. "You grew up a long time ago, Willy Mae, in the physical sense," explained Alma. "But something tells me *this time* you're leaving me for good."

Willy wrapped her mother in her arms and held her closely and tightly.

"I love you, sugarpie."

"I love you, too, Mama."

Chapter 4

"We've got ourselves a bus," declared Peter when he met Willy at the airport in Caracas.

Willy arrived in Venezuela wearing her raggedy jeans, a red, white, and blue tank-top, holey sneakers, and her hair pinned up under her brown floppy hat with Sonny Rollins tooting his horn through the headset of her Running Mate. She managed to pack all of her stuff into a duffle bag and carryall, which she had lugged on and off the plane and watched a thin-lipped security agent paw through for the third time since she departed from Tampa.

"Where's all your luggage?" Peter asked.

Willy smiled broadly to say, "This is it."

"When Char's traveling, she has two or three suitcases, a makeup case, garment bags, and all kinds of junk." Peter hoisted Willy's duffle bag over his shoulder.

"That's her, not me."

As Peter and Willy exited the terminal, a boy of about twelve or thirteen called out, "*Ojala, Macha!*" Peter was sure Willy heard it, but she didn't react.

"Where'd you get this thing?" Willy asked outside, upon

beholding the beat-up, retired school bus that Peter so proudly introduced. "Can you drive it?"

"Sure, I can drive it. I bought it from a guy Billy Velasco knows."

"The *real* Billy Velasco? The one who used to play for Baltimore?"

"Yeah," chuckled Peter. "He's the shortstop for James's team, the Maracaibo Marineros."

"Wow," muttered Willy, duly impressed. Then she asked, somewhat nervously, "Is it safe?"

"Yes, it's safe!" said Peter, slightly annoyed that Willy didn't share his appreciation for the bus's charm and character. "Plus, gas is unbelievably cheap down here." Peter, clad in sweatshirt, cut-offs, and sandals, was more appropriately dressed than the last time they saw one another. He was giddy with enthusiasm for the winter games soon to begin. He rambled nonstop for what turned out to be a three-hour ride. "You'll love the villa. It's right on Lake Maracaibo . . . We have this married couple, Juan and Marisabel, who take care of the place, do all the food shopping so we don't get ripped off in town. They translate and act as travel guides. Heck, we're really living in *their* house . . . I've got a contract for you to sign. Like I said, the pay is peanuts, but you might as well spend it all while you're here. It's a hassle exchanging Venezuelan money for US dollars, and you can't take the bolivars out of the country . . . We'll be eating a lot of rice and beans and beans and rice . . . There are six guys—well, seven, counting me—with some big league experience on our team. The rest are locals, but they've all played in the amateur league here in the summer. We've got four players from the Wolves with us. One kid from the Instructional League team cancelled out on me at the last minute. His name's Kevin

McDonald, and he was a high draft pick out of college last year, but the front office labeled him 'good field, no hit.' He couldn't handle inside breaking pitches. I worked with him and showed him how to get around and pull the ball the other way, and he's actually got some pop in his bat. He'll probably be in the Wolves' starting lineup on opening day."

Willy was weary from the six-hour plane ride, feeling hot and grimy, and the scenic inland highway lost its appeal after the first hundred miles or thereabouts. "How much longer?"

"About twenty more minutes," Peter said flatly.

"Ooh," Willy whimpered. "You gotta let me out to go pee in the bushes. I'm gonna explode."

When Willy returned from her jaunt in the underbrush, Peter said, "Maracay, where we play, is too far away to go back to the villa after our home games, and we'll probably have to sleep on the bus or in the locker room or something when we go to Caracas, Maracaibo, and Lara."

"Sounds just peachy," Willy smirked.

"And I was thinking," said Peter with noticeable caution. "Maybe you should suit up before we go to the ballpark. There's not much privacy."

"No way!" snapped Willy, who had been sitting directly in back of Peter but now came to hover over him as he drove. "I'm one of the guys. That's all there is to it."

"Whatever you say," Peter said glibly.

The villa was nothing fancier than a large, white stucco house with a veranda overlooking a grassy hillside adjacent to a short stretch of beach between some rocky shoreline. The lake water was still, the air was refreshingly cool, and there wasn't another house in sight. There Willy met Peter's four teammates from Buffalo, lounging around waiting for Juan and Marisabel, the caretakers, to return from town with food, whereupon they waited for "the wife" to cook it. There was plenty of time to get acquainted before tomorrow morning's practice session.

Scott Bruneau was a pug-faced and, to Willy, incredibly young pitcher who already had a year in the bigs under his belt. Scotty brooded about his life as a relief pitcher. "It's too stressed out. The pressure gives me gas."

Gene Tyler was a catcher who spent most of his ten-year-long career in the minors. Gene described himself as a red meat eating, truck driving, Christian Republican, but Peter whispered, "Don't worry about him. He's okay. He doesn't vote or go to church."

Peter introduced Alex Suarez as, "The unofficial assistant manager, translator, and utility infielder, but I'll probably stick him at second base full-time so he can argue in Spanish with the umps for me." Alex seemed to be a smart kid, displaying quiet amusement at the way Peter tabbed him to be the cultural advisor for the rest of the guys from the States, even though he had never set foot in Venezuela in his life.

Glenn Harmon, like Alex, was an infielder, only twenty-three and just arrived, but was more than a little homesick. "The front office encourages young players to get married. Then they turn around and send me out of the country to winter league after going back and forth between Buffalo, Wichita, and Niagara Falls for two years. I have a career, but not a life!"

Willy noted that Scotty, Gene, Alex, and Glenn were unexpectedly cerebral and introspective, not stereotypical jocks. Willy supposed they weren't necessarily indicative of the Buffalo Wolves so much as the kind of people Peter Jones would befriend.

Later, after Marisabel prepared whatever strange combinations of Latin and Anglo cuisine the guys wanted, Willy sat among the group and lectured everyone about the virtues of organic fruits and veggies as they chowed down. When Gene made a wisecrack about "wimp food," Willy downed six redhot chili peppers, two burritos filled with steamed vegetables, and a bowl of *arroz con frijoles* doused with "enough salsa to choke Cha-Cha Cepeda," as Peter put it. Then she challenged any or all to run a few miles with her and left to trot alone along the water.

Willy awoke the next morning, apprehensive about the day's workout with her new team. She rid herself of excess nervous energy with a quick five minutes of meditation, another run along the lakefront, and a steamy shower. *Get clean to go sweat, Willy!*

The field was a small, old-fashioned ballpark, similar to hundreds where minor league and semipro ball had been played since the mid-nineteenth century. The stands were recently painted but only ranged counterclockwise from third to first base. No seats were beyond the wooden scoreboard in center field and the fence that rimmed the outfield. A few of the local townsfolk, mostly noisy and antsy children, came to watch the ballplayers practice. As Willy looked down at her feet treading the brownish green grass surrounding the all-dirt infield, she turned her head skyward and felt a tingling. She hummed softly to herself, a melody without lyrics, and gazed at the sparse clouds tracing white against the blue morning sky. Papp had spent winter after winter playing in California, Mexico, Cuba, the Dominican Republic, and Venezuela. Willy felt as if she were shadowing Rube's footsteps, or maybe coming home and bringing his spirit with her.

When Peter had spoken earlier about the rest of the team, he had deliberately neglected to mention the other *bona fide* big league star on the squad. "Anybody look familiar to you?" Peter asked coyly.

"Merk!" screeched Willy, recognizing the tall, wiry fellow chattering loudly and smiling extravagantly with a handful of young players.

Mercurio Mercado evoked images of baseball icons of bygone days. The old-timers would say: "If you see Mercado play, you see Clemente and Minoso." Merk was all atwitter in the batter's box, ready to lunge at the ball and break down the line. "Say hey! Is that Mercado or is it Mays?" The perpetual smile on his face was a Chitown classic, reminding hometown fans of Ernie "Bingo" Banks and Slammin' Sammy Sosa. Willy thought last year's baseball card with Mercado wearing a Redbirds' cap seemed oddly out of place and he ended up having a subpar season in St. Louis after nine stellar years in Chicago.

Merk strolled over to shake Peter's hand, and, in turn, Willy's. Mercado immediately initiated a ribbing of his erstwhile rival turned teammate. "Buffalo Wolves, eh? When I read you're goin' to Buffalo, I'm thinkin' too bad he's gotta go back to the minors. He used to be good."

"We'll see who's playing in October, Merk," Peter said lightheartedly.

"*De nada!*" Mercurio Mercado told Peter Jones, "You can be a superstar in that league, P.J." Willy had already noticed some of the guys calling him "P.J." To the best of Willy's knowledge, his wife, brother, and father called him Peter and that was how she would continue to address him.

"As for the business at hand," said Peter, throwing a playful fake punch at Merk's chin. "All I know is, you're batting third and I'm batting fourth. We'll see what the rest of this crew can do as we go along."

"Why're you gonna play if you're the manager?" Willy queried.

"I'm not just here for the experience. I'm here to win," asserted Peter. "That's the best experience there is."

Merk brought one arm around Peter's shoulder and patted his stomach. "It'll keep you in shape, ol' man."

"Unless I get hurt," said Peter, rolling his eyes. "Then I'm up a creek without a paddle with the front office in Buffalo. So," he continued and pointed to Willy, "if the only way to win is for you to pitch a shutout and me or Merk to hit a homer, that's what we'll have to do."

Willy saw Merk's eyes widen and his ever-present smile fade. "No kiddin', eh?" he said, gesturing toward the willowy young woman while looking at Peter, who slowly nodded his head and smiled. "I thought she was your girlfriend or somethin'," Merk chortled and Peter could feel Willy's temperature rising at his side. Her fuming, however, wasn't so much in response to Merk's "girlfriend" comment, as Peter thought, but rather directed at him for keeping her presence on the team a secret. Thus, Willy gave P.J. a hard kick in the shins as she moved past him to take Mercurio Mercado by the arm.

Putting on her sweetest smile and softest voice, Willy said to Merk, "How about if I throw some to you?"

"Okay," he replied with a backward glance to Peter, as Willy led Merk toward the batting cage on the far side of the ballfield.

"She thinks she's a hotshot, Merk. Give her a good spanking."

Merk may have heard Peter's admonition, but the big league center fielder was rapt by the hotshot's jibber-jabbering about how her grandfather played ball in Venezuela fifty years ago. From a distance, Peter watched Willy throw batting practice for Mercado, which, needless to say, was no gentle serving of "bee-pee." Merk cursed, waved his arms, and slammed his bat down with every pitch, shouting, "*Basta, Willy Macha!* Enough, woman! Lemme hit somethin'!" Merk sliced a few line drives, but mostly whipped the air as Willy delivered each strike with a smile and a shriek. Finally, Merk tossed his bat aside and walked off with Willy, bantering gaily.

After meeting, most of the rest of the players, half of them locals, some of them only teenagers, Willy again heard herself called "Macha." She took Alex aside.

"Macha? It just means you're a tall girl . . . I mean, woman. It's nothing bad, but it's nonsense in Spanish . . . *macho, macha* . . . you can't make the masculine feminine."

"Some people think that about baseball, too." Willy joked.

Later in the morning, Peter pushed Willy to "go talk" to one of the other pitchers, Guillermo Alvarez, who was called Memo. Said Peter, "Having a bullpen and bench are luxuries down here. I've only got sixteen players and only five pitchers. If I use three relievers in a game or somebody gets hurt, who pitches the next day? So, be ready to go nine innings."

Willy's expectation that Peter would break her in gradually was not the case. Indeed, Peter decided to let Willy start the first game of the season against Lara. The only person more surprised than Willy was Memo Alvarez. Whether his big league career lay ahead of him or was finished greatly depended on his performance this winter. Therefore, he wasn't pleased at taking a backseat to a fledgling—and a woman no less!

Before the players began attacking a sumptuous outdoor luncheon spread, Peter opened up the boxes of uniforms.

The shirts were dark blue with "Medias Blancas" inscribed on the front. "All right!" yelped Willy. "We're the Maracay White Sox." She begged for number twenty-eight, explaining, "It's my birthday number," but, in fact, she wanted the number Rube Henry wore when he played at New York's Polo Grounds.

After lunch, the player-manager and designated hitter called a team meeting in uniform on the field, although the eight young locals on the squad wanted their traditional midday *siesta*. Thus, there was considerable bilingual grumbling as P.J. began his spiel. "We open up tomorrow at home against los Bravos de Lara. Good thing, too! Even if we beat them in Lara, it's no big deal, but we finish up the season in Caracas against the Q's."

"The who?" asked Willy, Gene, and Glenn in unison.

"The Caracas Conquistadores . . . the Q's!" pronounced Peter as several of the local boys intoned the team's nickname with reverence. "I just hope we're not fighting the Q's for the championship in the last week, because if we beat them, they'll have to send in the army to get us out of there alive."

"Are you serious?" asked an astonished Willy.

Laughed Merk, "Our fans are very enthusiastic. Ya know, real fans . . . *fanatics!*"

In the midst of groans, scoffs, and wisecracks, a chuckling Peter waved his hands. "Listen, this is a really nice country. The people are super. It just gets wild sometimes." P.J. ran through the league's three other teams, the Q's, Lara, and Maracaibo, managed by Jimmy Mack Jones. Peter joked about his brother having "four Japanese exchange students" on his ball club. "The only night games are played in Caracas and never on weekends. That's only like six games at night for us all season."

"We've got lights here, though," interrupted Willy.

"They don't work," Peter said glibly, adding, "Don't count on the toilets either."

"I already found that out," Willy complained.

Merk, sitting beside Willy, raised his arms in the air as he declared, "The woman's here one day and she floods the outhouse!"

"All I did was flush," she yelled, whipping off her new cap and hitting Merk's shoulder with it.

"You ain't supposed to *flush* the darn thing!" howled Merk, amid their teammates' laughter.

On the ride back to the villa, Jed offered to drive the bus and Peter relaxed, chatting with his housemates and teammates. "Why does Merk still play winter ball?" Glenn wondered aloud. "He's over thirty, a star. P.J., you're here to show you can manage a team, but he's got nothing to prove."

Alex leaned forward from his seat, directly behind Glenn's, and said, "He's Venezuelan. He's paying his dues, saying thanks."

Peter nodded agreement as Willy chimed in, "Did you see the way the young kids on the team followed every move Merk made, listening to everything he said?"

"Especially Lassie," said Peter referring to the big and strong young first baseman with soulful eyes and the eagerness of a puppy.

"The boy's name is Omar, Peter," Willy chided.

"Whatever," snickered P.J. in a good-natured way. "Merk's already taking Omar 'Lassie' Lazzaro under his wing. The veteran Hispanic players do that kind of mentoring of the younger guys up in the bigs, too."

"Merk's a good dude," someone said.

"I'm glad he came around . . . " Peter abruptly stopped

talking, but Willy quickly guessed she was the only one not privy to something that had happened earlier in the day.

"What?" she demanded of Peter. He shrugged with an embarrassed smile.

Alex turned to Willy. "He was going to quit the team. He wasn't comfortable playing with a woman."

"Merk?" Willy practically spit his name onto the floor. "Merk was gonna quit 'cause of me? After I threw him beepee! After we played and laughed together! After he was smiling in my face all day! That ugly sonofa . . . "

Willy quietly let the conversation move to another subject as she turned her head to peer out the window at the sparse greenery along the roadside. She clamped her teeth to keep her chin from trembling and drew long, slow, deep breaths through her nostrils to suppress a sob, hoping a tear wouldn't escape the corner of her eye to betray how hurt she felt.

Willy's outlook brightened upon returning to find Peter's brother, James, all settled into the villa. "Jimmy Mack" Jones wore a thick moustache and had happily dancing eyes, just like those of his father, Amos. Willy recalled the Afro of Jimmy Mack's playing days, when he was branded a one-dimensional good-hit, no-field player, not expected to rise above the Triple-A minors. Luckily he came of age in the era of expansion, where he stopped at every watering hole of diluted major league talent from Montreal to Tampa Bay and back again.

"Whatcha listenin' to, cuz?" asked James, harking back to the way in which Rube and Amos called themselves "cousins" to express a bond closer than friendship.

"My jazz," Willy answered, slipping out her ear buds. "I like classic 'modern' stuff like Trane, Dizzy Gillespie, Thelonius Monk, Miles Davis . . . "

"I'm an old soul man myself," James smiled with his twinkling eyes.

"That's how you got the nickname, right? That old Martha and the Vandellas' tune."

"Yeah," he chuckled. "When I got traded from the Brew Crew to Seattle, in my first game against my old team, I went four-for-four and they picked up on the line, *Jimmy Mack, when are you comin' back?'* They played it over the loudspeaker in Milwaukee every time I showed up to play there." James pulled a pipe and a packet of tobacco from his rear pants pocket, with a perfunctory "Hope you don't mind," to which Willy responded with a wink and a nod. "You should hear my wife, Katie, sing. She's got a sweet voice. She sings lullabies to the kids . . . Beatles' songs her mother taught her!" James laughed.

"I love all kinds of music. I'm not confined by labels." She added, "It doesn't matter if it's a piano concerto, rap, rock, hip-hop, or jazz. It's still music." James nodded as he sat beside Willy and lit his pipe with several rapid puffs and tiny clouds of smoke. "Peter said your ladies and the kids will be coming down here for Christmas and New Year's."

James beamed, "You'll love Katie. She's a freckle-faced redhead from Toronto with no hang-ups whatsoever. She keeps me grounded. You know what I mean?"

"I'd like to meet her. I can't wait to meet Charlene, too," Willy said.

James simply repeated, "Yeah, you'll love Katie."

Chapter 5

The mood in the locker room was light-hearted and convivial, as everyone was high in anticipation of the team's first game of the winter. At the ballpark, Willy gave Mercurio Mercado the proverbial cold shoulder, walking past his smiling greeting without response. Merk shrugged off her rebuff as probably due to "the woman's thing."

Willy undressed quickly and donned her uniform. With her blue cap in hand, she went to the row of sinks in the rear of the locker room and looked in the dingy, slightly warped mirror. She had worked out yesterday with a ponytail, but wasn't satisfied with the "look." She brushed her hair, picked it, combed it, twirled it with her bare hands, and brushed it again. She swept a part down the middle, clamped the brush between her teeth, and pulled two pigtails out to each side, letting them hang behind her ears. She smiled at the woman in the mirror. "That's you, Willy." She twisted an elastic band around each pigtail, put on her cap with a tug of its bill, and playfully blew herself a kiss in the looking glass.

The first game was at home in Maracay with 3,000 people in the stands plus hundreds more standing behind the low outfield fence, which was only 300 feet away and four and a half feet high. "Relax, this is just winter league ball," said Peter. Willy was so agitated she abandoned plans to run wind sprints and do some light exercise on the field. Instead, she remained in the dugout, pacing, sitting, jiggling her leg, unwrapping and chewing one piece of bubble gum after another, and all the while she babbled almost incoherently.

"What's the matter with ya?" Gene demanded to know. "You're makin' me nervous. Cut it out!" Then he grabbed a dangling pigtail and gave it a gentle tug, literally pulling her onto the field of play. "Let's go warm ya up."

The catcalls of "Macha!" began the instant Willy came within sight of the crowd. Game time was only moments away. She stood on the mound with Gene and pointed toward the front row of seats, draped in bunting resembling the Venezuelan flag. "Who's that sitting there?" she called to Peter.

"The owner of the Lara team," he answered, walking toward home plate. "He's some big-shot politician or something."

"Minister of the Interior," Alex clarified, as Peter motioned for his second baseman to join him as translator and cultural liaison officer for the perfunctory exchange of lineup cards with the umpire and Lara's manager, Oscar Valdez. Oscar, who had the countenance and personality of a bull rhino, was a journeyman first baseman and designated hitter in the majors and minors, but Merk colorfully described him as "a freakin' livin' legend with a left-handed catcher's mitt here at home." A loud and wildly animated discussion ensued among Peter, Alex, Oscar, and the umpire, Paco Avila, known as *el Jeffe*—"the boss."

Peter and Alex walked toward Willy, Gene, and Glenn,

standing as a group at the mound. The player-manager hailed Mercurio Mercado in center field. "I need all the help in Spanish I can get for this."

"What's going on?" Willy asked him.

"That mother-flunker, Valdez! He's talking some garbage about the official league rules not specifically allowing a woman to play."

"Flamin' idiot!" Gene cried, acting ready to throw down his mitt and fight.

Willy looked at Peter, who decreed, "It's just horse crap to rattle us or get us to walk off the field and forfeit."

Glenn Harmon asked, "Why can't we just sit Willy out for one game?"

Peter Jones, a shadow major leaguer's son, rebuked Glenn with a withering glance and the sharpest of edges to his voice. "You don't know where we come from, man. There's no way we're going down that road."

Glenn faintly mouthed an apology, not sure why what he said was so wrong, then forced a smile as Willy reached for his hand and squeezed it.

Said Peter, "We have to brain this one out." He squinted his eyes at the seats where the visiting dignitary sat. "I got it. Come on, Alex, Merk . . . ." A few minutes later, an exuberant P.J. returned to say, "When Señor Gonzalo Mendoza y Rojas runs for President of Venezuela, I'll be sure to come down and vote for him."

"What happened?" Willy asked.

"I told him . . . or Alex told him, I mean . . . I'd call every newspaper, magazine, and network in the States, and the bleeding United Nations, to tell all about the outrageous and sexist discrimination against a young North American ballplayer. Señor Mendoza told Valdez he'd better not embarrass his country in the eyes of the world that way, and Merk said it would be an insult to the modern women of Venezuela."

Willy turned toward Merk, who had returned to his outfield station, and caught his eye with a smile. He tipped his cap to her.

Said Peter, "Let's play us a ballgame."

The first Lara batter started off by calling time and jumping out of the box three times before Willy even threw the ball. Los Bravos' shortstop did a double-dutch skip on the first pitch of the game, which was a sidearm fastball headed directly for his kneecaps. He received the message, loud and clear, and settled down to business with no further attempts to unnerve the novice on the mound. The leadoff hitter grounded out, and the number two batter stepped up and dug in—and dug in and dug in. When el Jeffe signaled for the pitcher to deliver the ball as the batter was ready at last, Willy knocked him on his butt with an overhand fastball that whizzed past his ear. She jammed him on the second and third pitches, and hooked two curveballs on the inside and outside corners, effortlessly going from a three-and-oh count to a full count of three-and-two. The second-spot hitter swung and bounced out on the next pitch. Then the number three batter dug in and called time on Willy once more. Her reply was *jam! jam! jam!* followed by two swinging strikes, one on a slider low and away, the second on a fastball up and in. Los Bravos' third-spot hitter avoided striking out by popping a foul ball to the right of first base, and Omar reined it in with ease.

Returning to the dugout, Gene threw down his helmet, mask, and glove, and said, "That was the longest one-two-three innin' I ever seen."

Laughed Peter, "I think those guys will stop digging in on you from now on, Willy."

Willy nonetheless threw high and tight on the first pitch to every batter she faced. She enjoyed the excitement running through her body as the batter stepped back or swung in self-defense.

Willy was still steamed about Oscar Valdez's lame attempt to keep her out of the game when he stepped up to bat in the second inning. Hoping that Gene was on his toes, Willy tossed the first pitch at Oscar's wide back, the second at his protruding belly, and the third at his ample rump. With bat in hand, Oscar took three steps toward the mound, shaking off el Jeffe's attempts to grab hold of his arm. Willy had no desire to play jackrabbit with a huge bat-wielding gentleman after her tail. To Willy's surprise, Oscar stopped and said something beyond her limited Spanish to comprehend. Valdez gestured to Gene, who nodded and ran out to Willy on the mound.

"What did he say?" she asked Gene.

"He's talkin' English, Willy. He says cut the crap and pitch, woman!"

The first batter in the fifth rapped a hard grounder to Glenn Harmon at third base. Willy had thrown an off-speed, sidearm change of pace, about seventy-five miles an hour, which drifted over the middle of the plate. Clearly, she made a "mistake," but Glenn's glove work bailed her out. She struck out the two batters to follow. One looked at a slider hooking over the plate and the other swung at a slider breaking away. When Willy came back to the bench, she said to Peter, "I feel better now. I needed a couple of kays. They've been hitting everything."

A bemused P.J. looked at her and asked, "Are you in a

trance or what? You're going into the sixth inning with a flippin' no-hitter, Willy," he bellowed, then laughed, "and you're upset with yourself!"

Willy wrinkled her brows with high seriousness. "I know they don't have any hits off me, but I don't feel my rhythm yet. I walked two guys, including old Oscar."

Peter was still laughing. "Well, okay, try to work on your rhythm." Whispering to himself, he added, "And keep on doing whatever it is you're doing."

That inning, Gene Tyler shocked everyone, not excluding himself, by hitting a homer over the left field fence, sending the standing-room-only fans scurrying after the ball. Willy relaxed her concentration and, after notching her fifth strikeout, the next batter hit a low-and-away curve for a single with two outs in the sixth. The following batter popped out to end the inning. In the seventh, Oscar Valdez–"of all people," Willy lamented–smacked a long single with one out. Willy bore down to strike out the next hitter on three pitches, but walked the guy that followed. Overly cautious with the would-be tying and winning runs on base for los Bravos, Willy threw three straight breaking balls outside the strike zone to the batter at the plate. Sweat was dripping from her hair and Willy's shirt felt damp and slimy against her skin. She took a deep breath, closed her eyes, and fanned herself with her glove.

"Hey!" Alex yelled as he ran to her from second base. "Go right at him, lady. You whiffed him before." Then he swatted her butt with his hand. "So, toast him again!"

Willy fired an overhand fastball for a called strike and served up another heater. The batter's swing sent a fly ball to deep right center field. Merk backed up against the scoreboard–watching, waiting. He leaped at the last possible second and the tiny white dot disappeared into the pocket of his glove. Willy took a flying leap of her own, sparking the first sustained chant of *"Macha! Macha!"* from the hometown crowd. She pumped her fist skyward and sang, "All ri-i-ight!" She slapped every set of teammates' hands and buttocks that accompanied her off the field. She stood in front of Peter with her open-palmed hands held out and her feet dancing in place. "My first jam! Woo-hoo! Who's the girl?"

P.J. slapped her hands, and said, "You're the girl! Now, chill out. The game's not over."

The air was thick with the smells of fried dough, beer, and salsa. Kids stood on the bleacher seats, pounding out a staccato beat as three thousand voices rang out, *"Maracay! Maracay! Macha! Macha!"* Six batters later, with two outs and two strikes on Oscar Valdez in the top of the ninth, Willy unleashed a full-throttle fastball at mid-nineties velocity past the left-handed catcher's hopelessly late swing. Oscar looked stunned, bewildered. He said to Gene, "I don't effin' believe it. A woman! What was it, a two-hitter?"

Gene shook his head and smiled. "Ya should've stood in bed today, Valdez."

Peter rose from the bench to greet his newly found ace. For the first time in his fifteen-year pro ball career, he embraced and kissed a fellow player. "You made one hell of a first impression, Willy Beal."

Memo pitched the next day's game, throwing a five-hitter for the Maracay Medias Blancas' second consecutive 1-0 shutout over los Bravos. The entire team met at ten a.m. the next day at the ballpark to hop on the bus for a three-game series in Caracas. Las Medias Blancas arrived in Venezuela's capital city to find 25,000 fans on hand to view that evening's game against the Caracas Conquistadores. Willy nearly swooned as she gazed upon the assembled masses in Estadio Universitario de Caracas, which was the equal of any big league park in the USA or Canada.

"Relax, this is just winter ball," Peter repeated his saying, except that tonight they would play with an electronic scoreboard, music over the sound system, and a professional crew of grounds-keepers fixing up the field.

"And it's a hundred and ten degrees," complained Willy. "Phew!"

There was an elan to the Q's, a swagger in their step. They were very nearly the national team and it showed. The Caracas fans were exuberant, setting off deafening roars at every safe hit for the Q's and every snuffing out of Maracay. The home team thanked their faithful with five runs in the opening inning and went on to win, 8-0. After a night of sleeping in the visitors' locker room at the stadium, las Medias Blancas stumbled bleary-eyed into the next day's blistering heat, again falling behind in the first frame, 2-0. However, Maracay chipped away to take a 3-2 lead into the ninth. The Q's fans were shocked, then shattered, as a kid named Omar "Lassie" Lazzaro, who flunked his tryout with the Q's, hit a bases loaded single to make it a 5-2 game, and Scott Bruneau—"a nobody!"—struck out the side to wrap things up.

The loudest and noisiest crowd of the series flooded more than 30,000 strong through the turnstiles on the final day when Willy was scheduled to take the mound. Prior to her first game, Willy was hyper and worked off her anxiety by stinging Gene's palm, throwing the heater exclusively for her pregame warm-up. Today, Willy warmed up methodically, first throwing the curve, then the slider, and fastball five or six times, in turn, sidearm, buggywhip, and overhand.

In the first inning, the Q's lead-off batter began in predictable fashion, stepping out of the box to call time, stepping back in to crowd the plate, kicking up the dirt with his spikes, and digging in to distraction. Willy fired the first pitch sidearm at his wrists and buggywhipped the second at his elbows. Willy shot a third bullet down the middle of the batter's box for good measure, but the beleaguered man at the plate hit the ground as soon as she threw it. A shout of protest from the Q's manager drew a response in kind from Peter and was ignored by Paco Avila, again umpiring behind the plate. However, Willy missed the strike zone—or, perhaps, she was denied the ump's call—on the third pitch that followed and the opposing batter walked to first base on ball four. She would walk four in all on this day. "I think el Jeffe's strike zone done shrank," said Gene. Willy found herself working harder, and worrying more, than in her debut. Also, the Q's were more aggressive on the bases than lead-footed los Bravos. In the third, the runner on first kept stretching his lead, drawing a half-hearted pickoff attempt from Willy. The result wasn't a stolen base, but the intended distraction led to another base on balls. Then and there, Willy determined to screen out dancing base runners—and work on her pickoff moves with Scotty and Memo. Willy threw two pitches to end the inning unscathed by way of a foul out to third baseman Glenn and a bouncer to second baseman Alex for a textbook "twin killing."

The Q's jeering and riding of *la chica* on the mound was another annoyance, tempered by the realization that the tall *Norteamericana* had yielded only one hit in a dual-shutout with the Q's pitcher, Hector Cordero. The chatter fizzled with one, loud-mouthed exception.

"Who's that guy?" Glenn asked.

"Tommy—no relation to Oscar—Valdez," answered Gene.

"He just won't shut up!" Alex moaned. "We've bumped him, spiked him, and brushed him back and he's been sworn at in two different languages."

"What's he sayin' anyway?" Glenn asked Alex.

"Mostly stuff of a sexual nature. You know, shoving his thing into her thing. I don't think you'd enjoy it, Willy."

"I'll get him," Willy said cryptically. "Alex, tell Omar to stay on the bag at first, no matter what. Okay?"

Alex complied reluctantly, fearing that Willy would bean the unsavory character and assault him on his way to first base. Instead, she lobbed four pitches well away from the plate and Tommy trotted unmolested down the line. Willy readied herself to pitch to the next batter by going into a full wind-up delivery rather than working from the "set" or "stretch" position with a runner on base. Tommy "No Relation to Oscar" Valdez accepted the invitation to take a lead of several strides toward second base, all the while caterwauling about biting various parts of Willy's anatomy. He froze in place for an instant as Willy stepped off the pitching rubber and double-pumped her arm in an underhand, circular, windmilling motion to fire a 100-mile-an-hour death ray ahead of Tommy's diving slide, meeting his skull with a thud. There was stark silence throughout the stadium as Omar walked over to the motionless Conquistador, picked up the ball, and gently tagged him out.

"Oh, heck, Willy, you killed the dumb jerk!" Alex screeched. In the dugouts, the home team's manager marshaled his crew for a brawl of vengeance and the visiting manager plotted an escape route to get his team off the field, out of the stadium, and out of town. A moment later, Tommy's eyes opened and he pushed himself up from the ground. His face was placid, almost serene, as he unsteadily planted his feet and straightened up. He set his eyes on Willy and let out a horrible cry that sounded as if it came from the bowels of hell. He charged her, but was tackled, felled, and smothered by Omar and Gene. They held him in check and a protective ring of Bobby, Alex, and Merk, who seemed to have flown in from the outfield, surrounded Willy until an honor guard of Q's grabbed the arms, legs, and torso of "No Relation to Oscar" and carried him away, screaming and squirming.

Peter called time to talk to his pitcher. "It's a good thing el Jeffe already warned the dude to knock it off and now he's laughing so hard he wet his pants. You could've been tossed out of the game and maybe suspended. We got lucky this time, Willy." P.J. trotted past Avila on his return trip to the dugout. "They won't mess with my *chica* anymore. Right, Paco?"

The veteran of thousands of minor league and winter games, but who had never been offered a job in the bigs, rubbed the laughter-induced tears from his eyes and croaked, "La Macha's got balls!" Then Paco Avila's voice rang out, *"Jugamos!"* from one end of the stadium to the other. "Let's play ball!"

The Q's notched their second base hit of the game in the ninth inning, which ended on another double play started by Alex, with the score tied 0-0. In the top of the tenth, Maracay took a 1-0 lead and, in the bottom half of the overtime inning, a third and final one-base hit preceded Willy's fifth strikeout to end the game. The parting scene was the wholly unexpected sight of the Caracas fandom rising to its feet, clapping, and chanting: *"Macha! Macha! Macha!"* as the graceful phenom glided over the grassy playing field. "It's show time," someone remarked.

"You're kiddin' me," Willy said quietly as she doffed her cap, bowed deeply from the waist, and blew a kiss to the throng.

The next week, las Medias Blancas traveled to Lara, where they won two straight from Oscar's Bravos. On Thursday, the team bus with its crew of gritty, grimy, and cranky players returned to Maracay for a head-to-head match-up between the Jones brothers, a three-game weekend series with los Marineros. Maracay beat Maracaibo, 3-2, with Scott Bruneau again pitching well in Friday's game. Willy met Maracaibo's four "foreign exchange students" from Japan the next afternoon, just prior to the game she was to pitch.

Willy asked, "One isn't really Japanese, right?"

"No, he's Taiwanese," answered James, cupping his pipe's bowl and puffing, ignoring Willy's mortification. "His name's Hsu Xianxi," James sang. "We call him Shoe John Zee 'cause that's what it sounds like. He likes to chew tobacco, listen to gangster rap, and hang with the American guys."

With several players from both teams gathered, Willy bowed her head and shook hands with Hideki Saito, a pitcher, Toshi Hiayakawa, an outfielder, Eikichi Ike, also an outfielder, and Shoe John Zee, a third baseman. All four were rookies with the Watanabe Sailors of Yokohama. Eikichi had the best command of English, so he and Willy led the way in a boisterous and laugh-filled conversation. With the game due to start in a few minutes, Gene came to separate Willy from her new friends, still chattering with one another over their shoulders from afar.

"Motor mouth is running in overdrive," Peter snickered.

James shook his head in disbelief. "How'd she get them talkin' like that? Those guys don't say no more than yes and no and hello to me."

"She's . . . " Peter face strained, groping for the right word. "She's different."

James concurred by rapidly nodding his head. "She's a piece of work. That's for darn sure."

There was another packed house of 3,000-plus. "The paychecks won't bounce," thought Peter, who not only subsidized the American players' food and housing for the winter, but also paid for the team's new uniforms. The crowd was mostly children and half of them were girls. They were already stomping, clapping, and squealing, *"Macha! Macha!"*

Willy opened the game by whiffing Billy Velasco, Maracaibo's shortstop, on three pitches, igniting an early rise from the Maracay fans. She put down the side in order by getting the next two batters to ground out to short and third, respectively. James sent Hideki Saito to the mound for los Marineros. The tall, slender right-hander yielded two straight singles to Omar and Merk, who had also come through with two hits in Willy's second win. Hideki then bore down and escaped the inning without a run being scored. He cuffed los Medias Blancas through the ninth, allowing them to hit safely only twice after the first inning. Willy, too, blanked Maracaibo, not allowing a hit until the fifth. She gave up a second hit with one out in the ninth, which seemed to begin a game-winning rally until she blew away Velasco on strikes for the fourth time in a row. He dropped his bat on the ground, raised both arms to the heavens, and shouted something untranslatable. Thus, Willy pitched into extra innings once again.

"Let's see who makes a mistake first," said Willy, as she trotted to the mound for the tenth. With two away, Eikichi, who struck out in his initial at-bat, whacked a single through the hole at short. Willy gave him a congratulatory smile before feeding a curveball for Shoe John Zee to hit on the ground for an easy force out. In the bottom of the tenth, Glenn drew Hideki's only base on balls of the day, and Alex tagged a slow curve for a triple, driving in Glenn with the game's sole run. Willy, who had stared intently at the game in progress as her mates batted, promptly jumped to her feet and rushed onto the field to hug Alex and Glenn. She won her third victory, a three-hitter with eight strikeouts and no walks.

James told Peter, "She didn't throw nowhere near a hundred pitches."

"Eighty-five," Peter told James, "and sixty-five strikes." Then he added, "She's not only undefeated, but she hasn't even given up a run."

"Three shutouts! Wow! I'm doing good, huh?"

"Not half bad for an amateur," James replied.

The crew from the villa arrived at the ballpark early for Sunday's getaway game. James stayed at the park to sleep over with his players as a distinct coolness developed between the brothers Jones. Although today was Memo's turn to pitch, Willy went to the sidelines to throw for ten minutes to Scotty, the surrogate catcher. James and Peter stood together to watch her.

"She's even better than I expected, big bro'," said Peter. "Twenty-nine shutout innings! I will be so relieved when she gives up that first run. It's too much pressure."

"Oh, yeah, right," snarled James. "I feel real sorry for you . . . wonderin' if maybe she'll *never* lose a game." Peter laughed, but James was venting his frustration. "You say, let's go to Venezuela and play some ball, brother versus brother, our own fantasy challenge, just like when we was kids. Then you say you wanna bring ol' Rube's granddaughter with us, little cousin Willy Mae. You think she can pitch. Uh-huh! She's taller, smarter, prettier, and just plain *better* than any pitcher I got. Heck, half my guys are scared of her 'cause they heard from the Q's she'll knock your head off if you look at her funny. They think she's a witch or somethin' . . . And I'm supposed to feel sorry for you?"

Moments before game time, Willy delicately balanced herself atop the low fence alongside first base, attracting a noisy gaggle of children and teenagers, coming over to touch her hands, yank her pigtails, and kiss her cheek. Willy and the kids communed in a combination of Spanglish, sign language, and body language. When she withdrew from her young admirers, all pleading with her to stay, an elderly man reached for her hand, gently brought it to his lips for a fleeting kiss, and bowed gracefully. "*La Macha, usted es muy hermosa.*" Her tummy all jittery in response to the elegant gesture, Willy thanked the gentleman and departed behind the fence.

Maracay defeated Maracaibo for the third consecutive time. P.J.'s team was well in front of the league after winning nine of its first ten games. James's team was dead last. The tension between the brothers was evident, so Willy approached Merk and Billy Velasco about inviting the players from both clubs for a "bury the hatchet" party at the villa. The arriving guests found Willy in the kitchen, up to her elbows in cornmeal flour, with Marisabel, who was teaching Willy how to make tortillas by hand. "Hi, guys!" she said, scratching an itch and smudging pasty white dust on her nose. "Want lunch?" The mood was further mellowed by the ample flowing of beer, wine, and *cachira*—the favored drink of los Indios de Venezuela—which Hideki judged similar but inferior to *sake*. The evening ended in Willy's room, with

Eikichi, Hideki, Toshi, and Shoe John Zee burning incense and chanting mantras. "Some Buddha voodoo," James called it.

During the next week, la Macha y las Medias Blancas took on the Q's under the lights before another capacity crowd of 30,000 souls in Caracas. In the third inning, Willy's scoreless streak ended at 31-2/3 innings, when the Q's second baseman, Ronnie Dellarovere, a prospect in the Texas organization, laid into a buggywhip fastball. After giving up another hit, a single through the hole between shortstop and third, Willy retired the next nine Caracas Conquistadores in order, but with two outs in the sixth, Orlando Herrera, the Q's left-hand-hitting first sacker, connected with an outside-and-low fastball, sending Merk to the base of the center field wall for yet another of his patented jumps. This time the ball briefly dangled in the webbing of his glove before dropping over the top for the Q's second home run of the game, making it 2-0.

Peter watched Willy fling her cap, throw her glove, and stomp each article unmercifully. She clenched her fists, held them against her chest, looked upward and screamed. She did a little angry dance with her feet, delighting the crowd. Then she thumbed her nose at the home team's dugout and stomped around some more. P.J. made no move to take out his star pitcher. Willy's tantrum on the mound marked the last run and the last hit for the Q's. She got the final out of the sixth inning and retired the side, one-two-three, in the seventh and again in the eighth, beginning and ending the inning with strikeouts on "the slider from hell." Maracay put a scare into the Caracas fandom when Omar drilled a triple with two outs in the top of the ninth. The Q's veteran ace, Hec Cordero, intentionally walked Merk, and then Peter threw a scare into the crowd with a towering fly ball that just missed going out of the park. Thus, Willy was handed the first defeat of her professional career, despite pitching a four-hitter. However, her team would whip the Q's the next day and twice on Sunday, giving them a "safe" four-game lead halfway through the winter season.

Chapter 6

The villa was transformed from a ballplayers' bachelor pad to a family vacation resort as Alex, Gene, Scotty, and Glenn caught outbound planes to be with their families, and James and Peter trekked to Caracas to receive their mates and offspring disembarking inbound planes. Willy chose to remain at the villa, Peter's offer to pay her fare notwithstanding. Alma was angry as a hornet when Willy told her she wouldn't be coming home for the holidays, but she felt a strong need to connect with the other people in James and Peter's life outside of baseball.

Willy sat on the floor in the lotus, reading Nikki Giovanni's *Master Charge Blues* and listening to Mingus, when Katie Jones heralded her brood's arrival. "This is the invasion of the rug rats . . . Jimmy, Jeremy, and Amy. She's the *girl!*"

"That's what they say about *me* down here," laughed Willy.

"Howdy, I'm Kate!" She was tall, with cascading red hair, and enormously pregnant. As the three children swarmed around her legs, she thudded into a chair, her hands folded between her fully spread legs underneath her ankle-length dress. "Yesterday, it was buy stuff and eat. On the way to the airport . . . buy stuff and eat. At the airport in Toronto . . . buy stuff and eat. On the plane, at the airport in Caracas, and on the way here . . . buy stuff and eat. Phew! Good thing there's nothing to buy here! This is really a villa, is it? Is there anything to eat?"

The three munchkins stared at Willy. All of them had identical blue eyes, freckles, and reddish-orange curls. Amy wore glasses with inch-thick lenses, magnifying her wide eyes, and her frizzy hair was piled atop her head and tied up with ribbons like a bonnet.

"They're beautiful! I love their hair," declared Willy, as their father came into the room with suitcases, plastic bags, and a rag doll tucked under his arm.

"We keep sayin' we wanna start our own breed, but every time we hatch one, we wanna keep it," James proclaimed in jest.

"I'm the one who has the kids," said Katie, unselfconsciously rubbing her belly swollen with child. "James does baseball and sends home the money, but somehow I've been perpetually preggers for ten years."

Amy, the eldest at age nine, cupped her hand over her mouth to whisper in her mother's ear. "Dad was right. He said she was a pretty tomboy, just like me."

Katie acknowledged her daughter with a nod and turned to her husband. "There's a lot more to bring in, isn't there, baby?" James dutifully complied with Katie's softly spoken command and went outside. Amy, six-year-old Jimmy, and three-year-old Jeremy encircled Willy on the floor. The youngest scampered directly to Willy. Jeremy fiddled with her shirt and pigtails, but what he really wanted was a seat in her lap, which he had a moment later by simply plopping himself into place.

"Are you listening to music?" Amy asked Willy.

"Wanna hear?" Willy removed the headphones, which Jeremy was about to yank from her head anyway. Willy held both pieces to Amy's ear, letting her fingers brush against her thickly coiled hair.

Amy wrinkled her nose. "It sounds weird."

"It's jazz. What kind of music do you like?" Willy asked Amy, reaching an arm around her waist.

"The songs on the radio," she replied.

"I like the songs on the radio, too," said Willy, attracting the little girl's approval. Willy and the children now huddled, legs and arms entwined, on the floor.

She's amazing, thought Katie. *A kid magnet!* "Do you want a job? You can be our full-time nanny?" she kidded.

"Do you play baseball with my dad?" Amy asked.

"Well, I'm on your Uncle Peter's team," Willy answered.

"What position do you play?"

"I'm a pitcher."

"Oh, I like being the pitcher," Amy said. "Did you beat my dad's team?"

"Yeah," Willy answered slightly apologetically.

"You did? My dad's team is always the best. Awesome!"

"Oh!" chirped Katie as she noticed the wet spot left by Jeremy on the front of Willy's denims. "We're still working on the toilet training thing."

The woman ballplayer laughed and told Katie. "It's okay. Forget about it." Willy, Katie, and the kids became acquainted and downright comfortable before Charlene, Peter, and Peter Jr. came into the room.

"You could've told me that we'd be riding in that awful bus for another two hours."

"Sorry," Peter said to his wife.

"Did you find out if we can swim at the private lakefront out there?" she demanded in her smooth, full voice.

"Yeah, you can swim here this time of year," he answered defensively.

"Did you ask anybody? Have you seen anybody swimming?"

"No," came his meek reply.

"Hmm, that's what I thought. You knew I wanted to swim."

"Sorry," Peter repeated, but with a hiss in his voice.

Willy, anxiously awaiting the arrival of her mentor's spouse, practically tripped over her own feet to greet Charlene, who responded with a terse, "Hello, Willy."

"Can I help you get your things upstairs?" Willy asked her.

"No, thanks," said Charlene without making eye contact. "We can manage." Charlene returned her attention to P.J. "Did you set up a room for Peter Jr.?" The little boy wasn't exactly a toddler, but he acted it, clinging to Charlene's leg, sucking his thumb, and warily eyeing his cousins and Willy.

"I thought we'd figure it out when you got here."

"You didn't *think* at all." She wasn't the least bit embarrassed about displaying her anger.

Katie interrupted, "Petie can camp out in the room with our kids. We have sleeping bags. He'll have a ball."

"Oh?" The expression on Charlene's face softened.

Peter followed his wife and son upstairs, hauling five bags and suitcases clutched in his hands, slung over his shoulder, and dangling by a strap from his teeth. "Is she always like that?" Willy asked Katie, who shook her head. Then Willy added, "Kind of a chilly hello to me, wasn't it?"

Katie shifted her weight to one side in the chair. "Don't worry about it. Charlene's okay. She'll lighten up."

Willy later sat down with the blended Jones family to a hodge-podge supper prepared by Marisabel for a rambunctious party of nine. Peter Jr. was the only child dressed in pajamas, his father having gone through a half-hour wrestling and shouting match to get them on him. Junior immediately spilled milk on himself, sending the younger and elder Peters back upstairs for a rematch. After the fathers had ramrodded their tired and cranky brood to bed, Katie presented James with an early Christmas gift, five back issues of *The Sporting Times* he had missed since leaving Toronto. "The bible!" he cried in ecstasy. "Lukewarm off the presses from Saint Louie, Mo! Aw, Kate, I love ya," warbled James, as he fell into a chair and blissfully began reading.

Willy found herself awake and restless in the wee hours, and so she decided to get up, eat something, and go for a moonlight run. While chewing on a bowlful of rice with brown sugar and raisins, Willy scanned one of James's copies of *The Sporting Times,* happily discovering her own name at the top of the pitching statistics for the Venezuelan Winter League. Since she was a baseball stat geek herself, she checked the numbers of the leading pitchers in Australia, Mexico, Puerto Rico, and the Dominican Republic to confirm that her 0.49 earned run average was momentarily the best in the world. "Who's this guy Beal?" she imagined the baseball junkies back home saying. Then she heard shuffling little footsteps entering the kitchen from behind. She turned to see Peter Jr., wavering slightly as he stood with half-closed eyes, sucking his thumb with his forefinger crooked over his nose. "What's the matter, sugar? Can't sleep?"

"I'm thirsty," he said without removing his thumb from his mouth.

"I have some juice. Do you like pineapple juice?" Peter Jr.

nodded, still sucking and breathing loudly, barely able to keep his eyes opened. Willy sat him on her chair, fetched the container of juice and a cup, and pulled him onto her lap as he drank. One cupful was immediately followed by another. A few moments later, Charlene paused by the entryway to the kitchen, quietly watching and listening to her son being rocked in Willy's arms as she hummed a soft and low lullaby. At first, Charlene hesitated to disturb them, but asserted herself by clearing her throat. Willy looked up at her. "He's asleep."

"I should take him," Charlene said firmly.

"He's no bother," whispered Willy.

Charlene took a seat at the table with Willy, who was surprised to see the pack of cigarettes P.J.'s spouse held in her hand. "I'm a night owl," Charlene testified as she lit up and drew in deeply, then rose in search of an ashtray. "Most times, I wait for Peter to go to bed so I can smoke in peace. It drives him nuts, but he doesn't say anything. Sometimes I wish he would, though."

Willy changed the subject. "They're the same age, but little Peter is so much bigger than Jimmy." Willy withheld the further observation that he also acted younger than his cousin.

"He's going to be a moose. He'd eat twenty-four seven if I let him."

"Is he in first grade?"

"No, he's in kindergarten. We're moving to Buffalo . . . when we find a house, anyway. He wasn't school-ready when he was five and the trend is to hold back kids until they're six, especially boys. They're less mature than girls at the same age. I don't want him to be at a disadvantage."

Peter Jr. stirred in Willy's arms and abruptly woke to say,

"I have to go tinkle!"

"That's my job," chortled Charlene, dousing her cigarette and taking hold of the boy with a groan. "Say goodnight to Willy, Petie." Charlene directed him to set his feet on the floor, but instead he leaned toward Willy for a kiss, after which he withdrew to his mother's side and they left.

Christmas in Venezuela for the Joneses was a fair replica of holidays past, but Amy anguished over the absence of a tree and, more poignantly, pined for Granddaddy Amos, who was spending the day with his daughter, Betty. Willy, in the meantime, swallowed her guilt about abandoning Alma and rang her up on her cell phone for a long chat.

Ironically, the closeness Willy sought with Charlene as well as Katie was nurtured over the next ten days, just in time for their return home. On the final day of the family visitation, James and Peter were playing wiffleball—one of baseball's innumerable variations—with the kids in the lakefront sand. It seemed more like a touch football game with frequent shrieks and pile-ups. Amy broke away from the game on the sandy beach, shouting, "You always cheat, Dad!" as she came to visit her mother and Willy on the veranda. Amy went over to Katie and touched her stomach. The young one's eyes were wide and expectant as she laid her head upon what might have been a basketball hidden under Katie's white linen robe.

"Mom, I hear the baby moving."

"That's my stomach gurgling, sweetie."

"I wish I could hear the heart beating," said Amy, as she parted the front of the robe and pressed her ear against her mom's stretched out navel.

Katie looked at Willy, who was wide-eyed herself and smiling. "Katie, would you mind?" she asked with childlike anticipation. Katie shook her head, beaming radiantly, setting her orange-red hair swirling, and took Willy's hand. She placed it on her tummy and Willy rubbed, ever so gently. Katie seemed to enjoy sharing the moment of intimacy as much as Willy did. "Is that something?" Willy wondered, feeling a tiny nub.

"Let's see," Katie reached down and, without a hint of self-consciousness, lowered her shorts and felt around the spot marked by Willy's finger. "It's a little foot or elbow."

"Was that a kick?" Willy asked excitedly. Katie nodded. "That's so incredible."

"Yeah, it is," said Katie, still smiling, as she reassembled her clothing. After Amy had scampered away out of earshot, Katie winked at Willy. "Some men get turned off when their wives are pregnant, but I mean, James goes absolutely wild. I think my being preggers just makes him horny."

The two women were happily laughing when Charlene stepped out on the veranda, carrying a bottle of beer. "I want to get wasted," she announced with a crazed look on her face. She reached for the bottle of tequila sitting on a small, round table between Katie and Willy. "I know you don't approve," Charlene said to Willy.

"I'm not your mother," Willy said softly, smiling sweetly, with an exaggerated shrug of her shoulder.

Charlene giggled, then said, "A lot of therapists are recovering alcoholics, and a lot of clients prefer working with a therapist who's recovering. It's like a badge of honor. So, I let them think I am, but I'm not." She scarfed a shot of tequila and washed it down with a sip of beer. "I'm working with a special program for Iraq War vets and their spouses. The funny thing . . . or, I should say, sad thing . . . is that I'm still working with Gulf War vets. They have problems that never went away."

Katie rolled over on her side and turned toward her sister-in-law. "We Canucks are kind of in the dark about the world. You Americans are always going out on a limb . . . " She paused to finish off her own drink. "At least my kids won't get killed in some desert or jungle somewhere."

"James seems to be happy living in Canada," Willy observed.

"Yes, but he is *so* stubborn. He refuses to change his citizenship." She had been light-hearted, but added more seriously, "We both think the kids are better off. In Canada, nobody cares if they're black or white or biracial. In the States, they'd have to choose tribes . . . "

"It's not as bad as it used to be," Charlene interjected sharply.

"Canada was never *bad* to begin with," Katie retorted.

"Maybe we shouldn't talk politics, ladies," suggested Willy, and her two companions affably agreed.

"I'm sorry if I've been a little cranky," Charlene said to Willy, who feigned incredulity while guzzling a swallow of guava juice. "It's got nothing to do with you. It's Peter and me . . . it's always about *him*. Char gets lost. We're living *his* life, *his* dreams. What about me and my dreams? After all, what I do is important to me and the people I work with . . . but he's a ballplayer, famous person, blah, blah, blah! I make forty thousand dollars a year. He makes forty thousand a game!"

Said Katie, "You're rambling."

Said Willy, "Ramble on, Charlene."

Charlene's eyes shuttered and reddened. "For fifteen years, I've been waiting for his career to end so we can live a normal life . . . now we're moving to Buffalo. Next, he goes, 'I'm going to be a manager.' When's it going to end?"

Katie reached to clasp Charlene's hand and proclaimed to Willy, "See? One shot of tequila and she falls apart!" The three women laughed raucously, as Charlene wiped her eyes and nose with one hand and spanked her sister-in-law's knee with the other.

Willy chose not to tag along for the ride to Caracas, the first leg of the trip for Charlene, Katie, and their kids, since she became weepy just helping them pack and load their belongings. Saying goodbye to Amy was especially difficult, she and Willy declaring themselves soul mates and fellow travelers through the universe.

The games of winter resumed after January 6 with the Feast of the Epiphany signaling the end of the holiday hiatus. The next three weeks sped by, as Willy won three games, each victory following a loss for Maracay the previous day. She beat Lara, 6-1, on a five-hitter. This was the only time las Medias Blancas ran up the score with Willy pitching, but she was behind 1-0 until the fifth, after Oscar Valdez–"Who else?"–knocked in a run with a first-inning single. Omar hit an RBI-single to tie the game and drove in another run during Maracay's five-run outburst in the eighth. Player-manager Peter Jones looked like he got back his personal hitting groove, swinging the bat for a double, a run scored, and a run batted in.

At Caracas, four days later, in their third pitcher's duel, Willy stayed ahead of Cordero all the way, winning 3-1 on a four-hitter with six strikeouts. Hec pitched a five-hitter with five strikeouts. "Not too shabby for the both of ya," judged Gene.

Five days hence, Willy started her team's final home game against Maracaibo. Los Marineros managed a single in the fifth, another in the eighth, and drew a walk in the ninth as la

Macha hurled a three-hit shutout in which not a single base runner reached second base. In the winter's last doubleheader, Memo and Scotty pitched back-to-back wins against the Q's, clinching first place for Maracay with two games remaining. Peter gave Willy the weekend off. "Lay back and rest up for the playoffs."

With everyone at the villa hurrying about for the trip to San Juan for the Caribbean Series playoffs, Peter matter-of-factly informed Willy, "You, me, and James have to go to a banquet in Caracas tomorrow before we get out of town. I guess you're going to get a couple of trophies because you led the league in won-lost percentage, earned run average, strikeouts, shutouts . . . " He paused for effect, "Pitcher of the Year and . . . "

"You're kiddin' me!" she yelled hysterically.

"It seems your ERA, which registered 0.55, is an all-time record for Venezuelan baseball. They're giving you a plaque to that effect . . . " Peter was stunned to see Willy sobbing helplessly, her slender hands covering her face. "Are you okay," he whispered solicitously.

She mouthed "yes," but her voice wouldn't come out, as Scotty, the rough-edged pitcher, put an arm around her shoulder, placed the barest trace of a kiss on her forehead, and walked her out to the veranda. With almost comic clumsiness, Scotty raised Willy's chin with his finger, causing her to gaze down, rather than up, at him. "I don't think you're all choked up over them awards," he said. "You know how good you are."

She nodded and twisted her face in a distorted smile. "It's finished now. It went by so fast and turned out so good, but it's finished! I'll go home and read about you guys in the sports pages." Scotty knew not what to do or say, except to offer a hug, which Willy accepted and held for a few tender moments.

The banquet was a traditional Latin American midday feast. Willy arrived in a dazzlingly colorful sundress borrowed from Marisabel–taken in and lengthened; luckily, there was plenty of material to let down the hem. Willy thrilled the elite of Venezuelan sportdom, who expected la Macha to dress in her usual off-the-field tee shirt, sneakers, and jeans torn at the knees. She met the Minister of the Interior and owner of los Bravos in person, chatted with Orlie Herrera, on hand to receive the league's MVP award, and heard Paco Avila tell James that an independent minor league team in Salem, Oregon was looking for a manager. Willy spent much of the afternoon talking to Oscar Valdez–"of all people"–sharing a large tray of mangos, bananas, casabas, and plantains. Oscar, as she discovered to her delight, was a fellow vegetarian. "You never know about people," she muttered.

Chapter 7

The Jones brothers had made a deal that one would bring the other to the Caribbean Series as a coach if either of them won the Venezuelan championship. Their wives *sans* youngsters joined them in San Juan as well. "If the baby decides to come early, then I'd rather be in a strange place with James than at home without him," Katie said.

Willy was surprised at how casually Peter discussed raiding players from other teams for the tournament. James coming aboard as a coach was one thing, but using "ringers" seemed downright dishonest. The players P.J. wanted most were James's four Japanese exchange students, but they were already on their way to spring training with the Watanabe Sailors. Hector Cordero expressed interest, but later reneged, claiming visa problems. The sole ringer to come along to San Juan was Billy Velasco, giving Maracay a credible shortstop. Willy sat next to him on the plane ride from Caracas. He was ecstatic about having received an "invite" to spring training from Kansas City after being released by his former team.

"Hey, Billy?" She gave him a nudge with her elbow. "Are you excited about KC?"

"Call me Hilario," he gently corrected. "Yeah, I got a good feeling. They got Teddy Balin, their regular shortstop. He's good, but I can play, too."

"I'll say you can play!" assured Willy. "You're as good as anybody in the bigs."

"Oh, yeah? *Gracias,* Macha."

"*De nada,* Hilario."

The Caribbean Series was something of a preseason jamboree with baseball people—managers, coaches, would-be and used-to-be managers and coaches, scouts, front office staffers, and players—all descending on the tournament's locus. The first weekend in February was to be *"un buen tiempo."* After deplaning at the airport, Willy ran to a row of vending machines before she had even retrieved her luggage. She stood in front of a soda machine, fishing inside her carryall bag for loose change. "It takes dollars, Willy," offered a thoroughly amused Peter Jones, standing by to watch. Willy grabbed the newest, crispest George Washington from her wallet, slipped it into the machine, and wriggled nervously as she awaited the arrival of a can of caffeine-free diet cola, a pleasure she hadn't indulged since leaving Florida three months ago. *Punch! Clunk! Pop! Fizz! Chug, chug, chug!* "Aaah!" She sucked down all twelve ounces and punched up a second can. "You're going to burp all the way to the hotel now," said Peter, walking with Willy to the baggage claim area.

At the hotel, Peter summoned Willy, Memo, Scotty, and Gene for a meeting with James to go over the Mexican Winter League champion's lineup. Maracay would open the tournament on Friday against Jalisco, managed by Pat Salinas, a former big league pitcher. Aguayas, representing the Dominican Republic, was to play Arecibo, representing Puerto Rico, Saturday, with the two winners meeting in the championship finale on Sunday.

"We've got work to do," stated Peter, dropping pitching charts, batter's charts, statistical tables, and scouting reports onto a table. "No more winging it like we did in Venezuela. We do this thing like it's for real. The Mexicans are good, but the bleeping Dominicans . . . "

"They've got all three Walker brothers," declared James.

"Three?" wondered Willy, who knew of the two outfielders, Jorge of Kansas City and Domingo of Cleveland.

"Carmelito, the youngest one, is a shortstop in the minors. People say he might turn out to be the best player in the family one day," James explained.

"The Aguayas team also has Diego Santamaria," said Peter. "He's our catcher," meaning the Buffalo Wolves' catcher, which put a damper on Gene's mood.

Gene lamented, "Santamaria is the only catcher in the majors with a .300 lifetime battin' average. They just signed Jed Guerin as their backup. He's forty and he's been in the bigs for twenty years. The only reason he ain't in the Hall of Fame is 'cause he ain't gonna retire 'til he's dead. So, ya know what that means? I'm gonna spend the year in Wichita." Jed repeated with a pitiful wail: "Wichita!"

"Heck, the Dominicans could probably win the American East," chided James, eliciting a look of irritation from his brother.

"Can we get to work on the Mexicans? One game at a time, please!"

Peter explained that Willy would be the starting pitcher tomorrow with Memo ready to come on in relief if she ran into trouble before the seventh inning. Scotty would finish the game if Maracay was in the lead. For Sunday's final game, Willy could relieve Memo if he floundered in the early or middle innings. The obvious idea left unsaid was that Peter had no intention of using the team's other two younger pitchers. They were just along for the ride.

"Why can't I start both games?" suggested Willy, drawing five sets of raised eyebrows. "If we win tomorrow, that is."

"On one day's rest? That's crazy," dismissed Peter.

"You just said you might have Memo take over for me and me take over for Memo if you had to. What's the difference? He can be the closer and Scotty can set up."

"You can't pitch two games in three days," argued Memo. "You're not a machine, Willy Macha."

"I've pitched four games in a single weekend in softball tournaments," she insisted seriously.

"That was softball . . ."

"Peter," Willy said, a hint of irritation entering her voice. "You're going back to Big League Baseball two weeks from now. My little fantasy is played out. I've got all the time in the world to rest up."

Peter looked at James, who said, "She can probably go five or six innings anyways."

"We'll see," P.J. said quietly.

The next morning, Willy met Joanna Mercado and Pilar Velasco over breakfast with their husbands, both of whom were remarkably gentlemanly in their wives' presence. Except for stopping by Katie's and Charlene's respective rooms for quick hellos, Willy spent the better part of the day alone.

She went to Hiram Bithorn stadium three hours early and got inside by identifying herself with *"Me llamo Willy. Soy la macha de Maracay."* There was immediate recognition by the security guards and workers on hand; such was the level of interest in winter ball throughout the Caribbean. Willy threw to an invisible catcher and batter from the mound, kicking and stomping it so thoroughly that the grounds-keepers would never be able to erase all of her little marks. She would find them beneath her cleats at game time, marking "her spot." Willy ran wind sprints, stretched, and walked the playing field, covering nearly every square inch. She showered, changed into her uniform, and meditated on the locker room floor for twenty minutes by the time her teammates arrived. This was the most important night of her life and she was ready.

The glare of the lights and the din of the crowd were dizzying. Estadio Hiram Bithorn was a packed house of 35,000, with a few hundred prosperous Venezuelan baseball crazies, who loudly hailed *"Macha! Macha!"* when the name of las Medias Blancas' starting pitcher was called out over the public address system. Willy's pulse throbbed, her breath was short, and the rush of adrenaline numbed her legs as they glided over the grass in her dash to the mound. "She's hot," Peter Jones announced. She stung Gene's palm with five overhand fastballs for a quick warm-up. "She's hyper," an opposing player observed. She twirled her clenched fist in the air and shrieked, "Let's go! Come on!" She blew kisses "around the horn" to her infielders, Omar, Alex, Billy, and Glenn. The home-plate umpire laughed, "What a flake!" She did a little war dance around the mound, pigtails tied in flowing blue ribbons jiggling around her cap, and the crowd cheered. "I'll be darned. They love her already," said Jimmy Mack Jones.

Willy's eyes bore down on Jalisco's lead-off batter as he stepped up to the plate. She delivered the first pitch of the game with a piercing shriek and the right-handed hitter swung at a low-and-away slider for strike one. The batter saw her blazing eyes and heard her fierce scream again before his bat whipped under a sidearm fastball for strike two. Another down-and-out slider sliced away from the barrel of his bat for strike three. With two outs in the first, Willy threw a low sidearm fastball that was clubbed for a triple, but she jammed the next hitter, a young slugger named Henry Mullins, with a high hard one, getting him to bounce out to first base. The inning ended and she received a standing ovation as she ran from the mound to the dugout.

Maracay scored its initial run in the second when Alex Suarez socked a triple with his teammate-manager, P.J., on base after hitting a single. Jalisco's third baseman, a skinny fellow named Rudolfo Young, who played for Salinas's team year-round in Mexico, burned Willy with a two-base hit to open the third, but was left stranded as the next three batters popped, grounded, and struck out. Willy opened the fourth by laying a straight fastball over the plate for strike one to Mullins, who, like Orlie Herrera, was a big first baseman in the Baltimore chain. "You're mine, Henry," Willy whispered. Then she enticed him to chase a windmill fastball for the second strike and she spun him completely around with another underhand fastball for the third strike. She drew a second standing-O from the crowd and a warning from P.J., "Whatever you do, don't throw submarine to him again."

Maracay scored two more runs in the bottom of the fourth on four consecutive hits by Peter, Gene, Alex, and Glenn, making it a 3-0 game. In the fifth, Rudolfo again knocked a double off la Macha, but failed to score. In the sixth, with one on and one out, Mullins came to the plate. She recalled the scouting report that Mullins never swings at the first pitch and she remembered P.J.'s warning about throwing underhand. Big, strong, handsome Henry looked like such a fool when she crossed him up the last time that nothing could restrain Willy's arm from dropping down and serving another windmill fastball. As the bullet exploded from her palm thigh-high and arced toward the plate, Mullins measured its trajectory perfectly and powdered it off the center field wall for an extra-base hit that put runners on second and third. When Willy cast an eye to Mullins standing at second base, he smiled and wiggled his middle finger at her. She responded by waggling her tongue at him. She dared not look in Peter's direction, but she could feel the heat he was generating from the dugout. The runner from third base scored on a sacrifice fly by the next batter, whereupon Willy felt her own temperature rise. She let out an angry howl as she fired Papp's heater for the first of three straight strikes to the final batter of the inning.

The score was Maracay 3, Jalisco 1. Since Willy had escaped the jam created by her own playfulness, Peter offered a restrained smile and quickly retracted knuckle-bump when she returned to the bench. In the seventh, she fooled the lead-off hitter into popping up on a slider that broke in and failed to fool Rudolfo "el Magnifico" Young on a slider that broke away. He rapped it through the hole for his third hit in three trips to the plate. The next batter bunted Rudolfo to second. With two outs and a runner in scoring position, Willy uncorked the heater again: strike one, strike two, and a bat-splintering triple to the deepest cavern of the outfield. The player-manager told his brother, the bench coach, this was the second time that a line drive slipped past the reach of the former golden gloved center fielder, Merk, and a Jalisco base runner ended up on third. Meanwhile, Willy kicked the dirt, threw her hat and glove in the air, and spat on the ground. Gene trotted out to the mound and stood silently as she explicated every vulgarity in the English language with a few choice phrases in Spanish, recently learned from her pals, Velasco and Mercado.

"Are ya finished?" Gene asked. Willy nodded, eyes staring down at her feet. "Feelin' better?"

"Lots," she answered, head still bowed. Willy tussled with the next batter to a full count and then walked him. There were two outs and runners on first and third in a 3-2 ball game. P.J. stepped out of the dugout and onto the field. Willy knew why Peter approached the mound. The on-deck hitter was left-handed, and Scotty, a southpaw, was warming up in the bullpen. P.J. smiled, but said nothing as Willy glared, tight-lipped and standing stiffly. After she put the ball in his extended hand, he said, "This is how we play the game up in the bigs. The starter gets us to the seventh with a lead. We bring in a setup man to get out of the jam and later we bring in a closer to save it. They call that relief pitching." Willy smiled ever so slightly and inhaled the warm evening air. "Save something for Sunday, Willy," Peter said, with the manager's traditional pat on the butt for the departing pitcher. Willy skipped across the infield grass as her replacement's name was announced, but it couldn't be heard above the noise of the throng. The fans gave her a long and clamoring sendoff, moving from applauding and cheering to a deafening chorus of *"Macha! Macha!"* Willy was breathless and wobbly-legged, overwhelmed by the crowd's response, so much so that she barely waved to acknowledge it. She ducked into the dugout and buried her head against James's shoulder, letting the tears pour from her eyes, bleeding emotionally until drained.

"You're some kind of pitcher, Willy Beal," whispered Jimmy Mack.

As things turned out, however, Willy would not be this

night's winning pitcher. Mullins skyrocketed a home run off Scotty, tying the game at 4-4. In the bottom of the eighth, a noticeably hobbling Merk hit a monstrous triple into the gap in left-center and scored on Alex's sacrifice fly moments later. Maracay was back on top, 5-4. Memo came in to pitch and finished the game with a strikeout to get the win. Immediately afterward, a mob of reporters descended upon the Maracay White Sox locker room, ignoring the victorious manager and winning pitcher, and barked questions in Spanish and English at Willy, ranging from "Why do you mix overhand, sidearm, and submarine deliveries?" to "Are you married?" and "Do you have children?"

The next morning Willy chose to go "shop hopping," as Katie called it, with her and Charlene, rather than checking out the Puerto Rican and Dominican teams' pregame workout with the guys. Katie was in good spirits, although walking, sitting, or lying down was becoming more of a chore due to her pregnancy. She gave Willy a birthday card from Amy, colorfully written and drawn in crayon.

"This is so cute," Willy said, smiling down at the card. "I love the way kids write down the side of the paper when they run out of space. They're so free."

"Well, we left them home and *we're* so free," Katie sang triumphantly.

Charlene placed her hand on Willy's shoulder as they walked. Char wondered, "Willy, why do you wear a sports bra over the regular one? I'd think the other way around would be more comfortable."

"You can tell?" asked Willy, fiddling with her blouse.

"I can tell, sure," Charlene began to say, easily keeping up with the two taller women's strides. "But it's not as if you really need one."

"Oh, yeah?" shouted Willy, amused at the ribbing she had just been handed. She pretended to throw a slap at Char, who gave her a hug instead.

After their shopping spree, they unloaded their loot at the hotel and jumped into a cab to the stadium. When they arrived, Willy was besieged by a gang of excited young admirers, screaming at her and causing a near riot at the turnstiles. She was rescued by a crew of security guards and escorted to the front-row seats reserved for the Maracay contingent.

"That was wild!" Katie breathlessly declared.

"It scared the crap out of me!" Charlene moaned.

Willy was flabbergasted. "Nothing like that has ever happened to me before."

The main attraction of the game, besides deciding tomorrow's opponent, was Arecibo's pitcher, Phil Abruscato, a lefty, who would be playing with Peter and company for the Buffalo Wolves in the upcoming season. Phil pitched well for five innings as the fans' favorite, Arecibo, led 3-2 until the Dominican bats erupted for five runs in the sixth, capped by Domingo Walker's three-run homer. The outclassed team representing the host island came unraveled and ultimately lost, 12-3, their disappointed rooters leaving the stands half empty by game's end.

On the eve of the last contest between Maracay and los Gigantes de Aguayas, gangs of baseball folk invaded all the best eateries and nightspots in Old San Juan. Peter and Charlene, James and Katie, and Willy led an entourage to a very chic café, where they ran into several Dominicans, including manager Yo-Yo Fuentes, the Walker brothers, and P.J.'s new Buffalo mate, Diego Santamaria. The Mercados were part of the group along with Alex, whose presence was commanded by Willy. "You be my date. Stick next to me so I don't feel like a geek."

Phil Abruscato was at the café as well. He was understandably downcast about his losing effort, but he had a good winter season and felt primed for winning a job in Buffalo's starting rotation in the spring. Jorge and Domingo Walker and their wives were friendly and jovial, while their younger sibling, Carmelito, smiled silently. Diego's spouse did not accompany him. When asked why, he simply stated, "She's not here." Peter then asked Yo-Yo how Tito Melendez performed in the Dominican Winter League.

"Teet beat us two times, but he's not the same kind of pitcher he used to be. He throws the splitty and a screwgie, but no more hard stuff."

P.J. shrugged. "You have to make adjustments to stay competitive."

Yo-Yo nodded in agreement. Fuentes, a former big league shortstop and Hall of Famer, managed a team every winter, but his full-time job was being San Diego's chief scout for Latin America and the Caribbean. After giving Willy kudos for her performance in the series opener, he talked about the baseball camp he ran in the fall for kids in Costa Rica with San Diego's manager Leo Cortez.

As the evening wore on, the discussion became louder and even more dominated by game talk. The spouses, including Katie and Charlene, were neither lost nor disinterested. They knew more dugout politics and insider baseball than Willy imagined. They hadn't chosen their husbands' profession, but it was one with which they were intimately familiar. This was one night when Willy spoke only if directly prompted. She soaked up the ambience like a potion. The talk of strategy, players, and free-wheeling opinion from a gathering of living, breathing big leaguers was sheer bliss. "Nirvana," she said to Alex.

Charlene gently rubbed a finger between a few strands of Peter's hair. "You're getting some grey, honey."

Peter narrowed his eyes to study Charlene's neatly sculpted hairdo, softly falling in a wave across her forehead. "How come my hair keeps getting greyer and yours doesn't?"

She just smiled and cupped his calloused hand to kiss it. "What's on your mind? I can tell when something's up with you."

"I left three voice messages and an e-mail for Eddie Paris, the GM in Buffalo." Peter jerked his thumb toward Willy. "He didn't send anybody down here. We're going to come up empty handed."

"Not everything is about *you*, Peter," she scolded him.

"What do you mean *me*?" he hissed irritably. "I'm talking about Willy, making something happen for *her*."

Charlene's voice came quietly, but firmly. "You think she wants what you want for her, but you don't really know that. She may not want that at all."

With a smug grin, he whispered, "Oh, she does. It's the fire, Char. She's got the fire."

Willy was far less oppressed by the importance of Sunday's game than Friday's, which had been a preliminary for the team, but for her it was the supreme test of her mettle. She survived it and learned a lesson or two in the process. Today she would apply the skills she no longer needed to prove. Yet it wasn't just another game. An hour and a half before game time, she showed up at Charlene and Peter's hotel room and borrowed sundry cosmetics and a pocketful of jewelry, ready to pitch "dressed to the nines," so to speak, in lip gloss, eye shadow, necklace, bracelet, and dangling earrings. Aguayas was the "home" team as a result of a coin toss. The San Juan crowd was overwhelmingly tilted in favor of the Venezuelan team after the beating given to Arecibo the day before by the Dominicans. Also, the popularity of las Medias Blancas stemmed from a certain pitcher in pigtails. The mixed chants of *"Wil-lee! Wil-lee!"* and *"Macha! Macha!"* echoed throughout Bithorn stadium as she sprinted across the diamond, maniacally kicking the dirt on the pitcher's mound, and tossed her warm-ups. Yo-Yo called time and trotted onto the field, gesturing at Willy. The umpire came out from behind the plate and called, "Off with the bangles and beads, lady. They're distractin' the hitters." He plodded toward her as Peter approached.

"Aw, that's bull!" James howled from the dugout.

"What's up with that?" Willy protested.

"He can do it," P.J. said calmly.

"If Fuentes wants 'em off, they're off," ruled the ump, holding out his beefy hands to receive the jewelry.

Willy muttered, "Shoot! Curse you, Yo-Yo!" while carefully removing each glittering article.

"It's part of the game," Peter said soothingly. "Don't let it rattle you. Stay focused."

She leered into the Dominicans' dugout. The crowd booed and Willy sent the lead-off batter face first into the dirt with a cross-seam fastball thrown up and in at his chin. Message sent and received, but Willy walked Jorge Walker with one out in the first inning. As his brother, Domingo, stood at the plate, Jorge took a big lead and easily stole second base. A glare from Willy was Jorge's only penalty. Domingo dodged a brush-back and then struck out on "the best backdoor slider I've seen all winter." A tight sidearm fastball and two hooking sliders put Willy ahead of clean-up hitter Santamaria with a one-and-two count, but he connected on her next pitch, a buggywhip curveball, and sent it into the left field stands for a two-run homer.

Gene walked out to the mound to talk to Willy as Santamaria plodded around the bases. "Hey," her catcher said. "Don't feel bad. This is the guy I'll be playin' third string behind in spring trainin'. Remember?" Willy made no reply. "Listen," he continued. "Ya been callin' your own pitches all winter. I shouldn't've let ya throw him a curve. It's my fault."

"Forget about it," she whispered forgivingly.

The inning closed with a meek ground out, but the second frame opened with a base hit. Again, the runner on first took a long lead off Willy, who hesitated to throw over to Omar at the bag. Yo-Yo pinpointed Willy's weakness, but when the base runner sped to second on a one-one pitch, Gene delivered a fast and accurate throw to Alex to catch the would-be thief. The next batter sent a sharp liner to left center, beyond Merk's reach, and wound up on second with a double. Thus, the time had come for a deep breath and deeper concentration. Willy heard the fans cheering her on and tried to absorb their energy. Willy alternated offspeed fastballs inside and sliders away, and struck out the two batters that followed–six strikes on six pitches.

Aguayas sent a nineteen-year-old named Eugenio Enriquez to the mound, having used the ace of the staff yesterday. Said Merk, "He's fresh meat and we're the butchers." The butchers would get three hits. In the top of the third, Maracay got its first hit off Eugenio, but failed to score. In the bottom of the third, los Gigantes had another lead-off single, followed by a second stolen base. After Jorge popped out to Omar in foul territory, Willy struck out Domingo and Diego in succession, both on two-strike overhand sliders. Still trailing in the game, 2-0, Willy was sullen and angry as she returned to the dugout. Glenn wandered over and clapped her on the back.

"Lighten up, Willy. You just fanned two guys that hit over .300 in the majors last year," he told her.

"Yeah, I know," Willy said in a dull monotone, unsmiling, but her mood improved considerably when Merk took Eugenio deep for a home run, making it 2-1.

In the fifth, after whiffing Domingo for the third time, Willy threw an inside pitch to Santamaria, which he hit straight back to the mound. The hard chopper hit Willy full force in the chest, but she scooped up the ball with her bare hand and tossed to first for the out. Then she wrapped her arms across her ribs and fell to her knees, unable to catch her breath. There was a collective groan followed by utter silence from the crowd as several teammates huddled around their fallen standard bearer. Thirty seconds later, Willy flicked away the tears, stood up, and made her usual speedy jaunt back to the dugout amid frenzied applause from 35,000 well-wishers in the stadium.

Between innings, P.J. left the dugout and visited the front-row box seats to tell Charlene, "I didn't even know she was hurt. You know what she said? 'All I wanted to do was get the guy out.' Do you believe that?" Peter looked over his wife's shoulder and caught the eye of an old baseball man, seated a few rows away, whom he recognized. "The girl can't just pitch," he bellowed for the old boy's benefit. "She can *play!*"

Maracay couldn't manage another hit until the eighth inning and neither could Aguayas. After giving up a harmless base hit in the eighth, Willy finished her day's work with a dramatic full-count strikeout of Jorge. Her five-hit, eight-strikeout performance went down in the official record as a 2-1 loss after P.J. ended the game by taking a called third strike with a runner on first.

In the third row of seats behind the visitors' dugout, the old baseball man's stubby fingers held a blunt-tipped pencil, apparently scoring the game. The man turned to his companion, saying, "She blew away Domingo twice on sliders. One broke away and the other broke over the plate. The third time she fanned him, he chased a sidearm fastball he *thought* was a slider." He anticipated that pandemonium was an at-bat away—with Peter about to provide a game-ending hit or out—and so he rose to move toward the visiting team's dugout.

In the meantime, players from both teams crossed the field to congratulate their opponents. Willy made her way through what seemed to be waves of grabbing and pawing fans in the direction of the dugout sanctuary. There she found Peter and James standing with a tanned, older man whom they called "the Greek."

"I want you to meet somebody," beckoned Peter. "Manny Gabriel, this is Willy Beal."

She shook his hand and he said, "You did a nice job out there today. The other night, too. I saw both games."

Before Willy could acknowledge the compliment, she was besieged by a dozen media wags armed with microphones, video cameras, and voice recorders, and swept away for a bilingual "pool" interview. As Manny withdrew a pack of cigarettes from the breast pocket of his touristy-looking shirt, Peter asked him, "Who're you working for these days, the scouting bureau?"

"No, I'm freelance," answered Gabriel while cupping his hands to touch a match flame to the butt tucked in the corner of his mouth. "I go look at players when and where I feel like it."

"Baloney!" exclaimed Peter, laughing jovially. "You're working for Fabian, aren't you?"

Smiling wryly, Gabriel said, "Maybe, maybe not."

"Yeah, right!" quipped Peter. "What's the deal?"

The Greek shrugged his shoulders while sucking on his smoke. Then he eyed P.J. with unnerving intensity and asked, "So, tell me. How good is she?"

Peter Jones, the confident, controlled veteran, appeared pensive, even uncertain, as he watched Willy recite the lines in Spanish she rehearsed with Alex earlier in the day, thanking the beautiful fans in Venezuela and Puerto Rico for their kindness and affection. Explained Peter, "This started out as fun. Not a joke, but she's a super person and a great athlete. I thought she was good, good enough to hold her own playing winter ball. You know what I mean?"

First chuckling, then narrowing his eyes, Gabriel prompted, "Could she be the first girl in the bigs or what?"

Peter leaned into Gabriel's ear and whispered coarsely, "She's the best effing natural talent I've ever seen in my life!" If Peter were to say anything quite so unqualified and emotional to anyone, better it be to the chief scout for the richest franchise in baseball, the New York Diamonds.

When the scout rang up the general manager, Harvey Wanamaker, waiting in his Manhattan office, Manny would omit P.J.'s benediction; the best blankety-blank talent ever seen was routinely spotted by scouts on playing fields from New England to Nagoya, Japan. The scout didn't need to add any superlatives to the numbers Willy put up in the winter season and playoffs. Of course, scouts tend to favor taller players. His written report read, "This woman is a six-footer with a powerful set of legs." If a player fails to fulfill the promise, as most ultimately do, the scout can absolve himself by saying, "Well, he had the tools."

Manny told the GM, "She's got the tools, Harvey."

Wanamaker asked, "Can we get her with an invitation to spring training?"

"No, she's gonna get smart real fast. We better do a minor league contract. The scoutin' bureau will put her numbers into the computer and rate her as a prospect. Other teams aren't gonna wait for the June draft. If we want her, we gotta move *now*."

"Fabian said if she's good enough to pitch in the bigs, he wants her. Period!" the GM told the scout. "He says to pay her a straight thirty thousand dollars. If she smells the US Mint opening up, give her a signing bonus."

"Listen," the scout interjected. "Jones has some pull in Buffalo. He'll be talkin' her up to them. We could get into a biddin' war over her."

"All right, already," groaned the GM. "Fabian's willing to go to a hundred thousand."

"Uh-huh," grunted the scout. "Better fax me a standard fill-in-the-blanks contract."

"It's done!" said the GM. "Oh, and Manny? Make sure Jones isn't in the room when you talk to the girl. He's a clubhouse lawyer from way back."

"Mm-hmm," croaked the scout, noticing a mute pause on the line. *Fabian's been listening in on the call the whole time*, the Greek surmised.

Harvey's voice returned to life, saying, "Just make sure the girl doesn't leave San Juan unsigned."

Manny pretended to chuckle in amusement. "Do you expect me to tie her up in her hotel room?"

A clear, resonant voice cut into the conversation. "No, Manny, call my private number if anything goes awry. I'll come down there myself," promised Sebastian Fabian, the billionaire owner of the Diamonds.

"Understood, Mr. Fabian," Manny said as he hung up. He left messages for Willy at the hotel's front desk, on the phone in her room, and on her cell phone number palmed from one of her teammates. "This girl could fly out of town with a hundred grand in her back pocket before ever pitchin' an innin' in organized ball," he mused to himself out loud.

The female ballplayer who became the toast of San Juan would have enjoyed spending the evening with her friends—especially Charlene, Katie, Peter, and James—all of whom she probably wouldn't see for a while. Instead, Willy sat eyeball-to-eyeball with a balding, fifty-eight-year-old scout. Peter had coached her not to "grab the contract out of his hand and sign it," which was precisely what she wanted to do. He also suggested she let Manny think she had been approached by a team in Japan or Mexico. "Up the ante, if you can."

Willy sat erectly and poised alongside Manny in her hotel room with a coffee table before them. The veteran scout recited every passage of the basic contract and explained its meaning, although Willy requested no clarifications. He apologized that her working copy seemed to have more pages than the original because his portable photocopier handled letter-size paper, not legal-size, and he had to run through every page twice to cover all the text from top to bottom.

Willy leaned closer to Manny, resting her chin on her folded hands. She said, "That's sort of like a parable about the Symmetry of Life, balancing the *yin* and *yang*. No matter what you do, you can't get it all on the same page."

His vacant expression led Willy to believe that her cryptically abstract little joke flew right over his head. In fact, he was thinking: *This is no dumb chick from the sticks who just happened to learn how to throw a fastball, curve, and slider!*

"What if I get cut during spring training?" she asked him.

"You'll get one-sixth the salary, a month's pay," he answered. "If you get released anytime in the season, you'd just get paid what you've earned up to that point."

"There's not much security in that," she countered. "I thought the major league minimum was three hundred thousand."

"That's major league . . . "

"What's the minor league minimum?"

"There isn't one." Then he said flatly, "I think I can get the front office to approve a signing bonus, say, ten thousand dollars."

Willy nodded, openmouthed. "Sounds okay, I guess."

Manny produced a monogrammed pen and a checkbook, embossed with New York Diamonds Professional Baseball Club, Inc. The sight of it made her shiver and tingle.

"Let's wrap this up so's we both can get home," he said, trying to be friendly.

"Can I think it over for a few days?"

"Spring trainin' starts February fifteenth. That's next weekend, young lady."

The young lady bristled. "I've had inquiries from a team in Japan," she said, her words measured carefully.

Manny viewed Willy silently for a few seconds before saying, "Give me a break. Players go to Japan if they're washed up or can't make it in the bigs. Even if they offered you more money, you're not gonna pass up a chance to play in the real deal, are you?"

With the stroke of a pen, Willy's right arm became the property of the New York Diamonds.

Chapter 8

Sebastian Fabian built a billion-dollar sports, entertainment, and communication empire on the modest foundation of a multimillion-dollar import-export and real estate business that he inherited. He was determined to field the best team money could buy and, even before his Diamonds won their first pennant, there was talk of a dynasty. Fabian's ego was tempered by the soul of a traditionalist. Fabian's dream team would win in Big League Baseball, Inc., and the only place to play was New York City. The Big Town once again had three pro baseball teams, as it had for most of the game's history. Fabian billed his newly acquired Diamonds as "America's Home Team," supported by his radio, television, and cable outlets in the Big Apple and radiated out to the top 100 markets in the US via his Millennium Channel superstation. Ultimately, the Diamonds called Greater New York home because sharing a third of the pie in the biggest media market on earth was better than having a monopoly anywhere else. Also, with baseball's largest stadium capacity from New Jersey's Meadowlands, Fabian took up the challenge of drawing not two or three, but four million in attendance.

Fabian's game was about winning on every front.

Fabian hired the best and brightest "baseball people" and, in the style of Steinbrenner, Finley, and Veeck, the owner made himself part of the show. Although the general manager, Harvey Wanamaker, did the legwork to sign the off-season's most desirable free-agent, a left-handed pitcher named Bruce Jacobson, the owner was on hand to introduce him and his megabucks contract to the media corps. When the GM engineered a blockbuster trade over the winter to bring superstar shortstop Demeter Fortune to the Diamonds, the playboy tycoon announced the deal from his yacht, cruising Long Island Sound, as Harvey sat in his office doing the paperwork and fielding follow-up questions from the sportswriters. While Sebastian fantasized about his Diamonds winning it all, Harvey's job was to keep the talent flowing through the farm system and into the hands of Tom Vallery—the best manager Fabian's checkbook could buy—in order to win on the field of play.

Nonetheless, Fabian's Diamonds bore the name of a town that believed baseball's world championship series existed for the sole purpose of tickertape parades down Broadway. All the media hype and talk of a dynasty milled the expectation for America's Home Team to prove it was the best ball club in the world. Should they fail to fulfill their promise, the Diamonds might well be expected to apologize to their fans for losing.

The expectation to win was no less burdensome for the team itself. The New York Diamonds were the classic example of a team "one player away" from a championship "on paper." The Diamonds won 100 games and finished second in the well-balanced National East. A third quality starter or another potent bat in the lineup could have brought them from two games behind in the final three days of the season. During the off-season, the owner bought and traded for both the pitcher and the bat, adding them to a roster that already included two 20-game winners, Gil Douglas and Sandy Lee Danielson, a pair of all-star outfielders, Roy Burton and Andy Gilbert, and a Cooperstown-caliber second baseman, Calvin Bonham. Fabian boasted of "my three Cy Youngs" and "my four MVPs," but he, as much as the fans and the media, considered anything less than the league's pennant to be a catastrophic failure.

Willy was home in Saint Pete for four short days before reporting to the Diamonds' spring training camp in Deerfield Beach. She was in a tizzy all week, barely able to concentrate on unpacking from San Juan and repacking for the next six weeks. Alma was displeased about something. Willy was certain of it, but her mother was outwardly helpful and pleasant. When her daughter asked what was bothering her, she simply said, "Whatever do you mean, child? Why should I be upset about anything?"

The two local papers ran stories on Willy's signing with the Diamonds. "They seem to be downplaying the fact that I'll be the first woman ever to wear a big league uniform in spring training."

"Not when it was on the TV news, Monday, and not when that Sebastian Fabian was on *Wake Up, America!*" argued Alma. "They said it was a historic event, the beginning of a new era for women in professional sports, but they didn't say much about *you,* yourself."

"I missed all that! I was sleeping on the plane and running around the airport." Willy enjoyed a laugh until she noticed her mother's unsmiling face.

"Why didn't you call to tell me?" Alma asked frigidly.

"I told you about the phones down there and my cell's battery died . . ."

"Imagine," whimpered Alma, her voice unusually thin. "I have to hear about my daughter on the TV. My own daughter!"

Willy crossed the room to reach out for her mother. "I'm sorry, Mama."

"I love you, sugarpie. And I'm so proud of you, too," Alma said, welcoming her only child's embrace with a kiss on her forehead.

Willy placed call after call to New York, speaking with a dozen different people in the Diamonds' front office–everyone except Fabian himself and anyone that had definitive information on accommodations for new players. Finally, by Friday morning, she at least knew the name and address of the motel where she would be staying, so she rented a car on Alma's credit card and headed southward for Deerfield Beach. Willy packed an enormous bundle of reading material, all of it about the Diamonds: yearbook, media guide, a "dope book" of statistical minutiae, a preseason preview printed out from the Diamonds' "Home Team Home Page" on the world wide web, and *Sportsworld* magazine's special issue on the opening of spring training camp.

There was no question that the Diamonds were a ball club rich in talent. Demeter Fortune came to the Diamonds with the reputation of being the archetypical "I-me-my" ballplayer, selfishly more concerned with his personal goals than the team's performance. Fortune–a long-ball-hitting shortstop with speed–joined a lineup that already led the league in ego as well as expectations. The heart of the Diamonds' batting order was the "gold dust twins," Burton and Gilbert. They came up together as rookies five seasons ago and quickly began to rack up numbers that evoked comparisons to the game's greatest one-two punches, going back to the days of Babe and Lou or Josh and Buck. The home run and RBI totals of Burton and Gilbert were all the more impressive considering that they played in the Meadowlands, a cavernous "pitcher's park."

The acquisition of Cal Bonham, the best "little man" in the bigs, at five-feet-seven and 165 pounds, had two key outcomes for the Diamonds. His presence at the top of the batting order provided the speed and power of a true "sparkplug," and, as a ten-year veteran, he lifted the burden of leadership from the reluctant shoulders of Burton. Given the Diamonds' trio of "franchise" players, the highest salaried star was the owner of the signature on the most recently inked contract.

"Sorry, Roy," said Cal as the two men stood together to bond at the porcelain urinals. "No hard feelin's?"

"Hey, brother man, you got yours and I got mine. I'll catch up next time." *Zip!* "Right, Andy?"

"Yeah, same here, buddy." *Swoosh!* "Aaah!"

Enter Fortune, the shortstop with the silver bat and gold glove. At the tender age of twenty-four, the Diamonds' third switch-hitter still could go either way: to be a perennial batting champ—another Gwynn, Boggs, or Carew—or the next "40-40" man, hitting homers and stealing bases in equal measure. Besides fielding the position like Jeter, Nomar, or Ripken, Fortune had the foot speed to beat out bunt singles, especially when swinging from the left side, as well as to take advantage of the stadium's artificial surface, skipping grounders through the infield for phoney-turf doubles and triples. Yet, only in New York could Fortune win a batting title and fail to live up to his promise, as the fans and wags already framed his name within references to potentially hitting .400. However, the "smart money" was betting that Fortune would eschew a higher batting average to swing for the Meadowlands' formidable fences. Stud numbers, meaning homers and ribbies, bring the big bucks in salary arbitration and free agency.

When Demmy breezed into Manhattan for a preseason meet-the-media fest, he opened his mouth to sing the praises of an athlete quite pleased to be "me."

The *Journal*'s Brad Lucas whispered in a colleague's ear, "I love a guy who likes nothing more than talking about himself. They're more likely to get foot-in-mouth disease."

Lucas's chief rival, Dale Goodwyn, of the *Daily Mail*, switched off his miniature tape recorder and tapped Lucas on the shoulder. "We came here to throw darts at this guy to bring him down a notch, but you'd need a howitzer to punch a hole in that ego!"

"Welcome to New York, Demeter Fortune." Thus read the headline of *Today USA*'s weekly sports supplement, which Willy picked up at a truck stop, where she side-tracked to pee, gulp down a bottle of overpriced spring water, and pee again, on the final stretch of her sojourn to the New York Diamonds' training camp complex.

Diamond Town was a world unto itself, a big-time baseball colony tucked away in the southeastern Florida 'burbs. The Halladay Inn, about ten miles away on the main drag, and the Sheridan, directly across, were the enclave's satellites, housing virtually all of the unmarried minor leaguers and those who couldn't afford to put up their families like camp followers for a month and a half. The big leaguers generally owned or rented homes or condos in Deerfield Beach.

Players' wives and children, down on a quickie visit or for the duration of spring training, became more visible by the end of the first week.

When Willy set foot on the Diamonds' spring training complex, she shuffled slowly across the field where the exhibition games would be played and experienced the same illusion of *déjà vu* as she felt on her first day in Venezuela. The bluish green of the artificial turf notwithstanding, she was shadowing Rube's footsteps. "Your li'l gal's home, Papp." She shut her eyes and her sneakers became his cleats, the turf became sod, the Diamond Town field became Shibe Park, Forbes Field, and Griffith Stadium. Needles and pins chilled her shoulders as Willy Beal and Rube Henry walked together for a moment. The fully awake, conjured-up daydream wasn't at all eerie; it was as warm as the sun overhead.

Willy was surprised to find the manager himself greeting the nameless, faceless hopefuls and passing out their information packets with covers displaying the team's logo, gold ligature initials NY inside a blue diamond. Tom Vallery was the quintessential modern manager. Vallery ate quiche, spoke Spanish fluently, had an MBA, and relied on computerized tools to analyze performance and evaluate players. He simulated hundreds of games on his laptop during the winter months. Tom, analytical and scientific, was judged to be a "manager's manager," the role model and paragon for most of his peers.

Willy thought Vallery's neatly styled hair was thinner and greyer than it appeared from television and the sports pages. When Willy offered her hand for Tom to shake, he lifted it and turned open her palm, inspecting each finger with curious eyes. Then he smiled to say, "The length and dexterity of your fingers was highlighted in our scouting report along with your other vital statistics." He set her hand free, giving it a gentle squeeze. "Your fingers are God's little gift. Maybe there's magic in them. Let's see what you can do with it."

The pitchers and catchers reported to spring training on Monday, joining the rookies, minor leaguers, and nonroster players, followed by everybody else—the twenty-five position players on the forty-player roster—by the end of the week. There would be nearly 150 players in camp, more than 100 of them on the minor league side of the complex. Of the farmhands in camp, fully one-third might not be in baseball a year from now, at least thirty would be displaced by new draftees in June, and half of them would never play a single game in Big League Baseball. *Willy, you made it to a fantasy camp after all!*

Willy felt clumsy and self-conscious through a morning of clinics, classes, and mandatory reading aloud of handouts from Kristin Tracy, the team's VP for personnel, on sexual harassment, documentation of citizenship or immigration status, STDs, HIV, steroids, human growth hormone, and other banned substances. The luncheon spread in the clubhouse was too much of a carnivore's delight for Willy's taste. Plus she knew no one and couldn't remember their names when they introduced themselves anyway. So, she found a quiet corner outside to take a few minutes of meditation. Willy no sooner closed her eyes than she was jolted back to earth by approaching voices.

"Is that the girl they signed up?"

"Yeah, let's see what all the fuss is about!"

Willy opened her eyes to see herself flanked by two beefcake bookends. On a given day, the best pitcher in baseball was whichever one was standing on the mound. Gil Douglas and Sandy Lee Danielson—Dale Goodwyn called them "twin sons of different mothers"—were so similar in size, on-field temperament, and talent, but very different in style. Big Gil was power pitching personified, with arms, legs, and cap flying off the mound, reminiscent of his boyhood idols, Bob Gibson and Lee Smith. With the expression and intensity of a defensive lineman, Gil could throw all-out for nine innings if Tom would let him. He had a big slicing curveball, barely a ripple of a slider, and four out of five pitches would be fastballs. Douglas could put it over the plate or behind your ear and he relished being challenged by any hitter to a full count. Big Gil usually had the first and last word, and with runners on base he became still tougher. Like all the great power pitchers, Gil gave the batter something to think about besides hitting the ball.

At six-feet-eight in height, Douglas could have gone to the hoop with Shaq or LeBron if he had chosen basketball instead of signing with the Diamonds. Big Gil was the strikeout king, and Sandy Lee led the league in almost everything else, including wins, earned run average, shutouts, batters decked, umpires baited, and punches thrown. Whereas Douglas was mild mannered and urbane out of uniform, "the Rebel" was equally combative on or off the diamond. While every bit as awesome a presence as Gil, Sandy Lee was pure finesse in the details. He served an array of offspeed and breaking balls with pinpoint control. To contrast their styles, for Douglas, the ultimate perfect game would be twenty-seven strikeouts in a row; for Danielson, it would be twenty-seven infield ground outs—but he could strike you out with a white-hot fastball any time he desired, over any part of the plate. Sandy Lee, age twenty-six, was already a three-time 20-game winner, but held no illusions about himself and his place in the grand scheme of things. "If it wasn't for my arm and my eyes, I'd be lucky to get me a job drivin' a truck or punchin' a time clock somewheres."

Willy wanted to shriek like a groupie, but maintained her cool and offered a greeting, "Hey, what's up, guys?"

"We just come over to say hi," said Sandy Lee.

"It's our day off, so we're just hangin'," explained Big Gil. "We know they keep you rooks busy the first day. So . . ."

"We got more people to meet," Sandy Lee said to Gil, cutting him off. "The king is in the house. The messiah cometh."

"Aw, man, don't tell me he's here today!" Gil rolled his eyes and followed Sandy Lee's finger pointing toward the other side of the complex.

"And he's grabbin' Tom's ear right from the get-go."

"C'mon, Reb. Let's go make nice with the new guy. Catch you later, Willy."

In their wake, Willy correctly guessed that the king and messiah to whom they referred was Bruce Jacobson. The addition of the southpaw to the Diamonds' pitching staff gave America's Home Team *probably* the best "front three" in the bigs and *possibly* the game's top three individual pitchers.

There were mixed reviews of Jacobson's debut press conference at the Midtown Athletic Club in November. Goodwyn concluded that Jacobson wasn't the second coming of Sandy Koufax and "even more of a tool than I expected," but Lucas thought Fabian had struck gold. Indeed, the *Journal*'s ace writer was no cheerleader in print for the Diamonds, which he formerly dubbed the New Jersey Nobodies and now christened the Bergen County Carpetbaggers in light of the three big fish—Bonham, Fortune, and Jacobson—reeled in by the owner's deep pockets. After toiling in the bigs for five seasons, Jake scarcely won more games than he lost, while pitching for a mediocre team. Now, with the incredible machine of the New York Diamonds behind him, there was no limit to what he could do—or was expected to do. He had never won twenty, but the fans and wags asked, "Why not thirty?" *Welcome to the Big Apple, Jake. Good luck!*

The superlatives attributed to Jake dissipated when the discussion turned to his personality. Bruce Jacobson was known to be less than chatty with the wags, aloof toward fans, suspicious, critical, and unfriendly to teammates as well as hypersensitive to criticism from any quarter. Nevertheless, Jake was the new star in town. Goodwyn observed to Lucas over a brew, "Somebody ought to tell the dimwit this is the Big Apple. The fans here boo their own and don't take any crap from anybody. I can't wait until some loudmouth tweets him the morning after a bad outing and gives him some good old New York what-for."

Chapter 9

The equipment manager, Sheldon Kravitz, his North Jersey sallow skin grilled red from the first day of his annual southern tour of duty with the Diamonds, announced to the rookies and scrubs assembled in the clubhouse: "Those of you already assigned to Triple-A will wear the Jacksonville Jewels' uniform. The other minor leaguers and nonroster players get to dress up like New York Diamonds. If any of you stick with the big club for the regular season, you'll get custom tailored uniforms with your name on the back and your choice of numbers that're available, but for now you get what fits . . . and please don't crab about the numbers." Shelly Kravitz cleared his throat to deliver his soliloquy. "Listen up! I say this one time only. We honor the traditions of all five teams that've represented New York City. So, nobody—I mean *nobody*—wears number three, number four, number five . . . " He thrust his finger toward the group before him with each immortal number intoned. Some players stood bored and bewildered, whereas others registered recognition of every legendary numeral. The two guys closest to Willy listened as she invoked the names of the numbers' bearers:

"Ott and Ruth . . . Gehrig, Terry, and the Duke . . . the Yankee Clipper . . . " Shelly continued in the fashion of a herald of old: " . . . number forty-one . . . number forty-two . . . and number forty-four!" As if finishing a prayer, Willy whispered, " . . . Tom Terrific, Jackie Robinson, and Mister October."

Everyone was outfitted with four uniforms: home pinstripes, away grays, Sunday and holiday whites, and practice blues. The spring trainees were handed sets of cleats, jerseys, tee shirts, pants, socks, and athletic supporter. "I don't suppose you'll be needing one of these, Miss."

"Not in this life," Willy chuckled as Shelly wrapped a measuring tape around her hips, pulled it up, and cinched it at her waist. "I always wanted to be in a beauty pageant."

There was a sharp whistle and someone yelled, "Miss Meadowlands!"

She called out, "You better not say anything. Y'all hear me?"

"Hey, guys," someone jeered. "She needs a small ladies' top and a tall man's pants."

"Whoa!" sounded collectively.

Shelly said to one of his aides, "We'll have to customize a thirty-four long for her hips and rip out the waist band for her tummy, since we don't have any twenty-fours to go the other way and rip out the crotch."

"Ouch!" squeaked Willy in jest.

"Shoes all right?" Shelly asked.

"Yeah, men's sizes fit better than ladies' ones. I'm on the tall side, you know," joked Willy, peering down on Shelly's bald and scalded pate. He looked up at the smiling rookie. "If being able to take it and dish it out with these goons is any indication, it seems to me like you'll do just fine, Miss." Willy responded to Shelly's words as well as the sparkle in his eye with a wink. "She's as pretty as an angel, too!" he later told his wife.

As for locker room etiquette or protocol, most guys peeled off their clothing, stripped down to their jockstraps, hopped in and out of the shower, and hung around in the buff without giving Willy's presence a thought. At her physical, Willy's height, weight, and body fat were checked by the Diamonds' trainer, Mo Wallace. He was huge and carried too much midriff bulge for his job title, but the guys said he was "the best." Mo spoke to her coarsely as she sat astride the trainer's table. He held a two-pronged device in one hand and snapped his fingers at her. "C'mon, drop 'em! I can't use these meat hooks through your clothes."

Willy stood up and slowly removed her sweatpants. "I guess that's why my Mama always told me to wear clean underpants," she said with a wan smile, expecting him to ogle her hot red bikini undies.

"My God, you're built like a racehorse!" he shouted upon sighting her beautifully sculpted legs.

"You wanna see my teeth, too?" she said curtly.

Mo didn't respond, but went about the business of hooking the prongs around Willy's arms, thighs, and calves. He paused to give Willy an obviously exaggerated look-over. "You could set a new club record for low body fat, but you're way below average for a woman." This time she made no response as he nudged her to the scale, equipped with a moveable height measure. "You know you're actually six-two and an eighth?" Mo now seemed less threatening and Willy unwound a bit. "One forty-six and a quarter?" He raised his voice as if it were a question. "You've got a big frame, but you just don't look like you weigh *that* much."

"They say muscle's heavier than fat," she quipped.

Mo directed Willy back to the table where he began to press his fingers on various parts of her anatomy. "Any sprains, pulls, or tears I should know about? Old breaks? Hidden conditions?" She shook her head solemnly. Then the trainer smiled at her to say, "If half the guys on the big club were in as good shape as you, we'd clinch the pennant by the first of August."

"Thanks, Mo," Willy beamed.

Mo stepped away to peek into the next room and told Willy, "The doc'll see you in a minute." All Willy knew about Dr. Theodore Kyrokydes was that he was a surgeon whose specialty was arthroscopy and most of the players didn't fully trust him because he owned a one-percent share of the team in lieu of a salary. The doc was jovial and upbeat as he checked Willy's heart rate. "That's a distance runner's pulse. Strong and slow!" Willy was impressed that Kyrokydes drew blood samples and inquired about her medical history himself, instead of having an assistant do it.

"Do you have a primary care physician that you see regularly? We'll need to keep his name on file."

"I'll give you *her* name. My gyno's a woman, too," Willy asserted.

"Well, why not?" Dr. Theo laughed robustly. "Women are now the majority of students in med schools." Then his expression became more serious. "Please, don't be offended. I have to ask about . . . "

Willy was already exaggeratedly shaking her head. "No, sir! Nothing! Never!"

"Marijuana, hashish, cocaine, heroine, amphetamines, crack, acid, quaaludes, angel dust, PCP, meth, oxycodone . . . ?"

"Willy doesn't do drugs."

"Alcohol, nicotine, caffeine . . . ?"

"You'll see my blood work for yourself."

"Steroids, human growth hormones, blood-doping agents . . . ?"

"Nah-ah! No way!"

"Any family history of alcoholism, drug addiction?"

"No," she fibbed.

"Are you pregnant?"

"Nope!"

"Okay," Dr. Theo said calmly. "I'll tell you what I tell all the players. If a problem affects your play on the field, we better well deal with it, or else it'll mean your career."

"Thanks, I understand what you're saying," Willy murmured. She realized that Theo had discovered his own way to act out his fantasy in a white smock instead of a Diamond blue, gold, and pinstripe jersey. He was nonetheless on a team in the bigs.

Late in the first afternoon of camp, Rudy Judd, the Diamonds' pitching coach, and Lew Shankleton, the minor league pitching instructor, called a meeting for all the rookie and minor league pitchers. Oddly, the only sixty- and seventy-year-old coaches on the hip, slick, and highly polished New York Diamonds were in two of the most crucial positions. The presence of Shankleton and Judd, superb ballplayers in their day, reflected well on Tom Vallery's choice of people for his brain trust.

Lew Shankleton wore a crewcut of short, white spikes, his style unchanged since the onset of young manhood, Willy imagined. Shanks's face was deeply lined and the skin on his neck hung loose like a turkey's goiter. He was made of raw leather. "The big difference in the game today and the old days is relief pitchin'." Shanks's voice twanged with a coal miner's country accent. "When I came up . . . fifty odd years ago . . . y'know what they said? The same darn thing!"

Rudy Judd chimed in with his more mellow sounding voice. "This organization *develops* pitchers. We don't have no *brain-dead heavers* on the Diamonds . . . a brain-dead heaver is a guy who thinks changin' speeds means throwin' even harder, a guy who throws the ball at the plate and don't know where it's goin' to go. We teach pitchers to *think*. We teach pitchers how to use location and pitch selection as tactics in a game-winnin' strategy. In today's game, lots of the old rules are out the window . . . but don't ever forget that a pitcher's still a pitcher. The skills . . . "

"And the brains!" Shanks interrupted Rudy and tapped a finger on his forehead.

" . . . of a reliever and a starter work the same way," said Rudy. Then he and Shanks finished singing their tune in harmony: "You gotta know how to pitch."

There was a good deal of "hang" time on Saturday and Sunday between a light workout, playing catch and pepper, and a demonstration of the full-color video system that breaks down a pitch into hundreds of frames to show how the ball gains and loses velocity between the mound and the plate, how a fastball rises, how a slider curves, and how a curveball drops. Except for the manager and coaching staff, there were no big leaguers to be found until Calvin Bonham was spotted wandering the practice field. That he would be there, even though he didn't have to be, was totally in character. Willy leisurely exchanged tosses with Darnell Greene, the first friend she made in camp. Bonham walked briskly with one of the coaches, Silvio Romero, in the direction of Willy and Darnell. Cal wore an NYPD sweatshirt, cut-offs, and white high-top sneakers. He called Willy's name and offered his hand. "Good to have you aboard." Cal's handshake was forceful, but he followed it with a delicate pat on Willy's shoulder. "If you have some time later on, find me. We'll talk. Maybe go out, okay?"

Slightly awestruck, Willy stuttered, "Thank you. Uh-huh!"

"See ya!" Cal chirped. He was gone as quickly as he came.

"That was so nice!" Willy declared to Darnell. She was both touched and excited by Cal's gesture.

Darnell, meanwhile, began to dance on his tiptoes, wiggling and cackling, "Let's do lunch . . . oh, yes, let's . . . *la-dee-da*!"

"Oh, shush!" Willy took a playful swipe at him with her glove and he pretended to cower.

Willy met Cal Bonham "for a drink" in the motel lounge on Sunday night. Willy's "date" with Cal wasn't social, but she changed into a skirt and blouse, broke the seal on the unopened pantyhose, and put on her going-out shoes. She even wore lipstick, but the shoes hurt and the pantyhose itched. She kept forgetting decorum and scratched her thighs when she thought no one was looking.

"They said you were half a head taller than me, but I didn't believe it," he said upon greeting her.

"What else did you hear about me?" Willy asked whimsically.

"That you stole the show in San Juan," Cal said as they walked to a corner table.

"We didn't win the Caribbean Series, though."

"Doesn't matter," he laughed. "A lot of people are singing your praises . . . Yo-Yo Fuentes, Pat Salinas, the Jones brothers. Me and P.J. have been friends for years. Me and my ex used to get together with him and Charlene in Houston and LA."

Cal ordered a rum and cola and he nearly fell off his chair when Willy requested a pitcher of tomato juice with fresh lemon, pickles, olives, and celery on the side. She took the lemon straight, chomped down a stalk, and chased it with the juice spiked with black pepper.

"It's really going to be exciting with three such super athletes playing together," said Cal, citing Burton, Gilbert, and Fortune. "The thing is they're such different kinds of guys and types of players." Cal sipped his drink, darted his eyes around the room for a moment, and thoughtfully shook his head as he carefully placed the glass on the little cocktail napkin. "I'm tagged as a player with brains, so I could manage or go to work in the front office, but what I'd really like to do is broadcasting after my playing days are over."

"You'd be fantastic," Willy said enthusiastically. "Peter said you and he get along so well with the wags because you love the game's history, just like they do." Between careful bites of celery, Willy asked, "The Diamonds' pitching is gonna be incredible, don't you think?"

"Even if the big three stay healthy, that won't win us the National East," he said. "Three good starters and three good relievers, which we got, can win a best-of-seven series, but you need five starters to win the long season . . . and, believe me, it's long! Right now, the fourth and fifth starters could be a bunch of different guys up from Triple-A. Believe it or not, the best pitching staff in the league is shaky."

"You think Jacobson is as good as people say?"

"He's got the stuff. There's no doubt about it, but he's been a good pitcher on a weak team. Now he's got to prove he's a great pitcher on a good team. A really great pitcher makes a good team *better*. Gil and Sandy Lee do that. Half the time, I think, batters go to the plate against Big Gil and the

Reb with two strikes on them, *mentally*! Pure talent gets you to this level, but intelligence keeps you here."

Swallowing a mouthful of rum and cola with a wince, Cal continued. "I'm not into the numbers. This game is won by runs: runs scored and runs batted in. Those are the only numbers that count."

Willy's eyes were wide and bright, the tip of her tongue visible behind her parted lips, as she absorbed every word in rapt attention.

"You've got to be tired of hearing me talk."

"No, no, no!" Willy shouted embarrassingly loud.

"Yeah, yeah, yeah!" He mocked her, chuckling charmingly. "You talk now. How're you making out?"

"Not much has happened in two days," she began. "I only just met Douglas and Danielson for a minute, no chance to talk or anything. I do feel a little funny, but I'm not sure if it's because I'm a woman or just one of the new kids."

"Listen, half the guys on the team will *never* talk to you, not because you're a woman, but because you're a *pitcher*. To a hitter, the pitcher's the enemy, even his own teammates. Pitchers and hitters live in different worlds, Willy. Their skills are different, they think different, they see the game in a completely different light. Hitters are up there to get hits because it's their job, but pitchers see a safe hit as a *mistake*. Some guys do get friendly, though, like Roy and Gil or Andy and Sandy Lee. Now, I'm the kind of guy who can stay friends with actually anybody, but, mostly, pitchers and hitters just can't relate."

Willy reached for Cal's hands and enveloped them with her slender fingers. "Are we friends?" she crooned softly.

"Yeah," he said dryly. "You're pretty cool for a pitcher."

Cal and Willy chatted about baseball, past and present, for

another hour. By nine o'clock, Willy's eyelids began to droop and she started yawning. It was time to run, meditate, and hit the sack. She bade him goodnight with a handshake, sleepily scratching her hip at the same time. Upstairs in her room, she tossed the itchy pantyhose into the wastebasket.

The next morning commenced with a hundred well-conditioned but lethargic cranks running through jumping jacks, push-ups, sit-ups, isometrics, calisthenics, flexibility exercises, and freestyle aerobics paced by techno rhythms on a boom-box in front of three female fitness instructors. Willy planted her fanny on the ground and sat with back straight, hands on hips, and legs together. She pulled her torso forward from the waist by reaching for her right ankle and clutching it with both hands. She laid her head on her unbent knees and swiveled it to one side, then the other. She drew her trunk back up to center and repeated the stretching routine, this time turning left.

"Holy jeez! Look at her! How'd she do that?"

Willy did a full split, rolled over onto her side, and began to show off with scissor kicks. "What's the matter, you guys? Afraid you might break something?" her voice rang out joyously.

"You got that right!" answered someone. "There's more to life than baseball."

"True," she crowed. "But nothing's better."

"That's because you never had *me*."

"You'd do me good, huh?"

"You better believe I would."

"No way, José!"

"My name's not José. It's Tim."

"Nice to meet you, Tim. I'm Willy . . . Hey, you're pretty flexible, Tim. Try this!" Willy propped herself on her fingertips, raised a leg in the air, and stretched a single thigh muscle by pointing back with her toe.

"You gotta be kiddin'!"

"C'mon now! You can do it." Willy was barefooted. "Take off your shoes, so you can concentrate on your big toe."

"What? Okay! Uh, uh . . . *whew*! Like . . . this . . . you mean?"

"Yeah, you got it."

Later, Willy reflected that Tim Langevin, the Diamonds' left-handed "set-up" reliever, was one of the least likely players to have initiated her first big league ribbing. As Larry Brooks, the other side of the team's relief pitching coin, the right-handed closer, said to her, "Tim broke the ice with ya. A lotta guys didn't know what to make of ya. They didn't know how they was supposed to act."

"I'm just a player who happens to be a woman, Larry."

"Yeah, but they never had no woman *here* before. After that mornin', guys said 'she's okay' and stuff like that."

"I became a real person, huh?"

Larry huffed, smiled, and said with great seriousness, "Cal says ya act like ya were born on a ballfield. Guys respect him. If Cal says you're cool, that means you're cool."

Thereafter, Willy noticed greetings, banter, and conversation moving toward her rather than around her. Larry talked about a tinge of tendinitis. Willy took the opportunity to place her hand on his shoulder, consummating a friendship by touching. Larry spoke of the angst of life as a relief pitcher, sounding exactly like Scotty Bruneau, except that Brooks had solid credentials as a big league closer. However, Willy knew from following the team's recent history that Larry had alternated two brilliant seasons with a couple of mediocre ones, and whenever he warmed up alongside Tim, he knew he was partnering with his own permanent replacement. "You're only as good as your last outing." Willy walked alongside Larry as a group of minor leaguers approached, having just concluded a base-running clinic. "Say, brother!" Larry said to the tallest of the players.

"Another year with the Dukes!" the tall young man announced.

"They be callin' ya, man," Larry assured him. "Once ya get to Triple-A, you're as good as a Diamond!"

"Just a hamstring away . . . " said the tall player's diminutive sidekick.

Larry introduced Willy to Maxwell Street. "Wha's happenin', homegirl?" Max pulled his companion by the arm. "This here's Adam Bielski. We call him *the Psycho* . . . 'cause he's a psycho."

The Psycho stood with his hands thrust down into the pockets of his extra baggy, low slung uniform pants. "What up, Daisy Mae?" Adam the Psycho moved and emoted like a rapper when he spoke. Willy laughed sharply. "It's Willy Mae . . . and you're a character. Why do you talk like a street kid?" Willy wondered.

"Say what?" The Psycho swiveled his neck and thumped a fist to his chest. "I'm the real deal, girlfriend. If ya don't believe me, ya can squeeze me."

The odd couple, Street and Bielski, were late-round draftees struggling to stand out from the ocean of prospects, made up of more than a thousand players drafted every year.

"This year we're startin' in Alexandria, but we'll be in Jacksonville by June or July and maybe New York in September." The Psycho grinned impishly, saying, "Anything can happen. We just play and wait for somebody's ankle to snap."

Max clapped his hands and cried, "And it's hello, Broadway!"

Chapter 10

"Pitch with your legs, not your arm!" Rudy Judd admonished Willy during her first session of throwing a hundred pitches for twenty minutes with the pitching coach and Lew Shankleton standing on either side.

Said Shanks, "Think of the names . . . Seaver, Koosman, McGraw, Ryan! They all came out of the same organization in the '60s. None of 'em had a sore arm and all of 'em lasted 'til they was forty."

Rudy clamped his hands firmly on Willy's hips from behind, saying, "Put your weight here, not on your back or your shoulders or your arm." Shanks and Rudy watched Willy deliver a pitch. "She plants her right foot real good after releasin' the ball," Rudy said.

"Throw some sidearm," Shanks told her.

"Amazin'!" said Rudy. "Every sidewinder I ever saw took a clumsy lookin' sidestep to square himself after the pitch. She's smooth as butter!"

"That's because I'm female," Willy turned to say. "My center of gravity's in my butt, not my shoulders." She slapped herself and gave a little wiggle.

"Now, change up on the fastball, honey," Shanks ordered.

Willy held up her hand showing her fingers gripping the bottom seams. "I'm throwing a four-seamer. I change speeds by changing my delivery. The overhand's a little faster than the sidearm and the buggywhip's a little slower on the breaking pitches, too."

"You're gettin' mid-eighties velocity on an offspeed sidearm change-up? Your scoutin' reports said you could hit the low nineties. Let's see a straight fastball!"

"It's not that much faster," protested Willy. "I'd throw a two-seamer over the top maybe five or six times a game in winter league, but the batters who waited on it crushed it, and if I throw harder, I lose some of my control and sometimes it goes flat."

"Well, you let us be the judge of that." Rudy ordered, "Let's see what you got."

With each consecutive toss, Willy swiveled her hips further from the plate, craned her neck a shade more severely, and showed half, most, and all of her backside by the third or fourth fastball thrown. The more Willy coiled her body, the higher she kicked her left leg, and each successive pitch showed an incremental increase in velocity.

"Holy mackerel!" Lew exclaimed. "She can break a hundred easy."

"With the action on her pitches, she don't hafta throw no harder than she's doin' to be effective, Lew," said Rudy, his massive arms folded across his barrel chest.

Shanks shrugged and Willy said, "I can cross 'em up with the cutter instead of a change-up." She whirled and released a cross-seam or "cut" fastball from her over-the-top delivery.

"You're graceful as can be, sweetheart," said Rudy. Willy showed the two men her marvelous smile before throwing another cut fastball, this time sidearm. "It's still got that lively little kick to it," Rudy told Shanks.

"And she don't give nothin' away, neither," Shanks told Rudy. "You can't tell the delivery 'til she releases the ball and you can't tell the pitch 'til it's comin' into the plate."

Rudy called out: "Did your grandpa teach ya to throw a screwball?"

Willy stepped off the rubber, twirling the ball with her fingers. "He sure did, the fork and the splitter, too, but they don't work for me."

"You know the difference?" lanky Lew inquired.

"Of course, I know the difference between a forkball and a split-fingered fastball!" Willy snickered and pursed her lips. She tucked the ball between the bent knuckles of her forefinger and middle finger. "Fork!" she sang and tossed the ball into the air. She caught it with a slap against her palm and held it out again with two fingers forming a vee over the top seams. "Split!"

Shanks's wrinkly face glowed. Then he said coyly, "Let's have a look-see. Throw it!"

"But I can't get my good action and control on the splitty and my fork is slower than slow!" she whined.

"Stop bellyachin', honey," laughed Shanks. "You're here to learn."

Forty other fledgling pitchers were throwing their hundred pitches. For all of the young arms to have their day's workout would take four hours with the two coaches observing each for about five minutes, but Rudy and Shanks had spent a full twenty minutes watching over Willy. Shanks asked Willy to show her screwball. She threw the screwgie overhand, buggywhip, and sidearm. "What else can she do?" howled Shanks.

"What can't she do?" Rudy countered with undisguised wonder.

Shanks leaned over to Rudy, screwed up his mouth and cupped his hand over the former all-star catcher's ear, as if to share one of the universe's great secrets. "Rube Henry poured out thirty-some years of pitchin' experience and she soaked up every bit of it," he said. "And she's got the brains and the arm to use it."

By the end of the first week in camp, Willy began to feel happily comfortable. She fit in with her peers, position players and pitchers alike, everyone settling into a routine—but then the "others" showed up, the veteran Diamonds, no less than bubblegum cards come to life. The mood among the spring trainees changed to "us and them": *the big shots and the rest of us.*

"We're the people from the wrong side of Diamond Town, the rooks and the scrubs. Them dudes are the show!" said Psycho Adam Bielski. "We're nobodies!"

Most of the big-name Diamonds made their first appearance on Friday or Saturday, followed by media and print stars of equivalent magnitude: Lucas of the *Journal*; Goodwyn of the *Daily Mail*; the Millennium Channel's telecasting duo, Cameron Hammersmith and Jeff McCarty; and Dave Warren from USTV in New York.

Vallery and the GM called a team meeting for one o'clock on Saturday. For eight days, all the pitchers, catchers, rookies, minor leaguers, and nonroster free-agents *were* the New York Diamonds, but two-thirds of those players weren't invited to today's meeting. The only Diamonds' luminary not yet sighted was Demeter Fortune. Fortune's face was square-jawed and angular, his eyes were like cold blue steel, and his reddish blonde hair was short on top and longish in back. He could have been a rock star on stage, a young Jagger or Bono, Willy imagined. His body language delivered the message: "I am Mr. Wonderful." At least, that was the act he turned on and off in front of the eyes, mics, and cams of the media. In the clubhouse, he greeted and joked with his new teammates before suiting up and going to work: ninety minutes of solitary batting practice with the pitching machine; an uninterrupted half-hour powwow with Vallery and batting coach Chuck Walters; a session with the interactive full-motion-video pitching simulation system; an improvised workout of sprinting and jogging; to wrap up his day's labor, another hour of bee-pee with the bullpen coach, Hank "Handy Man" Froelichs, pitching, and Walters standing at Fortune's side, "observating."

Each morning for the next week and a half, the major and minor leaguers joined to loosen up by forming two rows and playing catch. A chorus line of players tossed little white balls back and forth, a ritualistic routine of unknown origin and uncertain purpose. However, the scene attracted scores of onlookers—vacationers, retirees, children, teenagers—peeking from behind the fence that ringed the practice field. Willy stood next to the most experienced pitcher on the staff, whose normal facial expression seemed to be one of bemusement.

"You're Steve Filsinger, right?" Willy said gaily.

"You're the girl, right?" he said, gawking comically.

As they laughed together, Todd Strickland, the minor league pitcher who paired with Willy to throw, went to find another partner.

"Why does everybody call you the guy next door?" Willy asked Zinger.

"I'm the nice guy that everybody likes, although I'm a little more choosey about reciprocating."

Along with Larry and Tim, Filsinger completed the Diamonds' bullpen trinity, the middle reliever and bulwark of the bullpen. Zinger was a sinkerballer, adept at getting ground outs and swinging strikes in the dirt. In his thirteen-year career he had handled every role a pitcher could play, from long and short relief to starter and stopper, playing on six different teams before coming "home" to New York–New Jersey.

"You like Rudy and Shanks?" Zinger asked Willy.

"They are so sweet," Willy sang.

"Sweet?" Zinger croaked. "Ask anybody who slid into Rudy Judd blocking the plate thirty or forty years ago if they thought he was *sweet*!"

Willy laughed and unconsciously adjusted her cap, shifted her weight from right foot to left, and fiddled with her pigtails. Zinger was taken by the graceful elegance of even such casual movements.

"You can learn as much as you need from Rudy and Shanks," he said. "More especially later on in the season when you need to work on certain things. Now, they're really only watching you, seeing what you can do." While Zinger spoke, Willy carefully slipped her fingers inside the vee neck of his Diamonds' tee shirt and lifted out the gold chain. "Don't strangle me, kid!" he cautioned, but moved not a muscle to stop her. Willy pulled the chain toward her, letting the Star of David gently spin in her palm.

"It's so delicate," she whispered, "for a big dude like you."

Zinger silently watched Willy as she tucked the gold chain back into his shirt, curiously absorbing the easy intimacy with which she touched him.

"It's funny," she said. "Watching a ball club on TV, you'd

never guess who the nicest people are gonna turn out to be."

"Yeah," sniffed Zinger. "You mean Cal, don't you?"

"How'd you know I was talking about him?"

"He's already been talking about *you*, that's why!"

"Oh," she said, surprising Zinger yet again by shyly averting her eyes.

"Listen," he said, giving her a manly slap on the back. "If you need help with anything, you should let me know. If it's something too complicated for me, like a woman's issue, I'll call my wife, Michelle. She already told me she wants to meet you. Okay?"

"Okay!" After a brief moment of silence, Willy said, "Would you show me how you throw your sinker?"

His face lit up. "Yeah, sure," said Zinger, picking an idle ball off the ground and tossing it to her. "I've got a knuckleball and a palm ball, too." Willy crouched like a catcher to receive Zinger's throws for about five minutes, shooting back at him a stream of questions about his grip, delivery, action, and location. Then he said, "Your turn, kid!" and Willy pitched to Zinger, although he knelt on the ground, due to his chronic back soreness.

Several yards away, Big Gil nudged Sandy Lee. "Let's go check out the lady."

Willy tried to screen out the distraction of the two studs bantering nearby as they watched her serves, but Zinger noticed that she had quickly switched from warming up to pitching. The overhand slider came in straight then cut away to his right. The sidearm slider came up and to his left then broke directly in front of him. The overhand curve sailed in hard as did her bottom-seamer fastball, which visibly jumped in midair. Another fastball came in with more movement and velocity than Steve Filsinger had ever been able to put on a ball in his big league career.

He mumbled to himself, "Who is this girl?"

Finally, Gil and Sandy Lee disrupted Willy's throwing to ask about how she controlled the slider, how she located it with respect to the plate, and if the change of speed with each delivery motion was intentional. Her heart pounded. Willy stuttered and stammered as she stood with wet armpits, rubbery legs, and goose bumps, talking to the two best pitchers in baseball, the twin pillars of the Diamonds, both of whom she idolized and tried to emulate. *They're asking me about my slider, no less!*

Mid afternoon, Willy was throwing pitches under the watchful scrutiny of her tutors, Rudy and Shanks, when she heard a voice say, "Let's take a look at the chick." She peered over her shoulder and saw Paul Cello watch as a three-quarter overhand curveball skidded off its mark. "Wild pitch, rookie!" he chided with a grin.

"You would've collared it, I bet!" Willy replied with no hint of humor in her voice. *I'll show him,* she thought.

The Diamonds' first-string catcher was dressed up like game day: plaid sweatband, tousled hair, two-days' growth of stubble, and sleeves raggedly cut at the shoulders. Only later would Willy discover that the ruffian, Paul Cello, and the wholesome fellow, Zinger, were the best of friends. Paul watched without comment, smiling sheepishly as Willy tossed several more pitches until Shanks yelled, "That's enough now, honey. Go and cool down."

Paul approached. His gaze hadn't lifted from her since he first came. Instead of a greeting, he said, "Who's the best hitter in the league?"

"Huh? I can't say for sure. There are four pretty good ones here . . . " She started to name Burton, Gilbert, Bonham, and Fortune.

"Forget about 'em! Ya aren't gonna pitch to nobody wearin' the same uniform. Who else?" he snapped impatiently.

"Kirk Tatum in LA, Tony Ortega and Eric Jackson in Frisco, Mercurio Mercado . . . " Willy was caught off guard and he made her nervous.

"No!" He shook his head with annoying self-assurance. "The best hitter in the league is the one who's comin' to the plate *next* . . . late innings, close game, men on base. He's the one who can *beat* ya." Cello put one fist on top of the other as if holding a bat. "With this!" He touched two fingers to his temple. "Or this!" His brown eyes shone radiantly now, as Willy relaxed and listened to his voice ebb and flow from loud to soft. "It could be some stiff in a playoff game whose only homer all season wins the pennant."

Paul was sorely in need of a haircut—his dark curls jutted out from under his sweatband and cap, over his ears, and down the nape of his neck. *Get yourself a comb, at least,* Willy mused. Yet, like Cal, Paul had no trouble eyeing the taller woman straight on. He also treated Willy forthrightly, putting his hand firmly between her shoulder blades and pushing her in the direction he wanted to go. His body language exuded gender equality with a shove.

"Kirk Tatum?" he muttered. "Ya can kill Big Tate with sliders if they break outta the strike zone. He can't get around with the bat and pull it the other way. He sucks anyway."

"Why doesn't everybody just throw him sliders, then?" the young pitcher asked the seasoned catcher.

"Because, if it's thrown up so that it breaks into the strike zone, he murders it. Plus, if it's a lefty throwin' to a lefty, it'll go down and away, right in his wheelhouse." Then Paul said, "C'mon, let's play some catch." Paul quickly sought and found a mitt, stooped behind his cap—"make-do for a plate"—placed roughly sixty-and-a-half paces from the woman in pigtails, and began calling the pitch, delivery, and location in a full, booming voice. He also gave each throw a grade: good, real good, not bad, and "lousy." Willy labored more strenuously in her ten minutes of working with Paul than she had since camp opened. There was a telekinetic exchange between pitcher and catcher as Paul called one pitch, then another. A progression, a pattern, a crescendo, and a musical score emerged. This catcher was the conductor who anchors the team, quarterbacks the fielders, and "handles" the pitcher. Willy was the pianist fingering the notes, chords, rhythm, and melody from the keys. The tempo rose to its symphonic climax and ended with flourishes. *Wow, I feel like he just made love to me!* When they finished, Willy was hot, tired, and wholly exhilarated. Paul said goodbye and she felt herself hating to see him go.

Willy's favorite part of the day was late afternoon, as activity wound down, when she wandered the clubhouse or the locker room, crunching an apple or a carrot, looking for a conversation to join. Willy found Max and Psycho talking to Darnell and Dino DeSantis, last year's and next year's solution to the Diamonds' "perennial center field problem," respectively. Willy's passing by and shooting the breeze in the clubhouse was how she met most of the veteran Diamonds. Roy Burton sat inside his locker cubicle, clad in only boxer shorts, with both hands clutching his left knee. "It's either my ACL or my MCL. If it's a strain, I'll be okay to play. If it's torn, my season's toast!"

Andy Gilbert offered Willy his stool when she came to visit him, but she plopped down on the floor in the lotus position instead. "The fans in New York take it way too seriously," Andy lamented.

"I wanna play anyplace where two or three million people come to see you play and, if you lose, they forget it by the time they hit the freeway," said big Joe Manlius, a slugging first baseman, from the next locker.

"The true fans love the game as much as their home team," said Keith Whalen, a third baseman in the "hot corner" tradition of splash and dash—make the play look hard by doing a belly-flop to field the ball and throw out the runner going to first while on your knees. Thor Andreason, the lefty swinging half of the Diamonds' first base combo, fielded the bag like a left-handed infielder and hit for average rather than power, an oddly anachronistic skill set for the position. Benny Marquez was notable for two reasons: he was the only Puerto Rican on the roster, an embarrassing anomaly and public relations *faux pas* for a team representing the City of Greater New York, and he was the former regular shortstop displaced by Demeter Fortune. *How good are the New York D's?* Like Joe and Thor, Benny would be a benchwarmer and role-player at the Meadowlands, but could be a star playing anywhere else in the bigs. *That's how good they are!*

The trainer's room was the Reb's domain. Sandy Lee sat on the table, his legs swaying as they dangled off the edge, his arms folded, and his head tilted in sync with the country ballad that filled the room with sound. Willy stopped in the doorway. He nodded to her and then closed his eyes to mime the lyrics of the tune, expecting her to walk on by. Instead, Willy strutted up to the table, hopped onto it, bent her legs into the lotus and sat right next to him. "Hi, y'all!" A look of shock and surprise registered on his face for a few seconds. Willy turned her head to the portable CD player blasting from behind them as the song changed. "Yeah, country swing!" she shouted with a broad smile and an approving nod.

"I would've figured you'd be coverin' up your ears and runnin' away from anybody singin' country. I heard you listen to jazz and classical and stuff."

Willy gestured with a sweeping wave of her hand. "Country's got soul. Willy loves her jazz, but all American music comes from the same blues and gospel roots. Brother Ray Charles sang country. Did you know, Louie Armstrong and Hank Williams used to jam together? I bet Elvis and Sam Cook and Roy Orbison and Otis Retting all sang the same songs when they were little boys in church!"

"Don't forget, some powerful ladies sing country," Sandy Lee drawled.

"Believe it," Willy bounced as she danced in place, seated beside the Rebel. "Where you from, Sandy Lee?"

"Stone Mountain, Georgia," he said. "Don't you read the publicity Mister Fabian spends all that money on?"

"You're kiddin' me!" squeaked Willy, manhandling him again. "My grandmother was from Dalton, Georgia. She was Wilhelmina, but they called her Minna. I'm named after her, but she passed on before I was born."

"Dalton, huh?" he said whimsically. "Maybe we're cousins."

"Could be, Sandy Lee." When Mo entered the room, loading up a syringe with cortisone for the most valuable right arm in the bigs, Willy jumped down from the table. "See you later, cuz."

As Willy disappeared from the room, Mo asked, "You hittin' on the Iron Maiden? Good luck, fella!"

Chuck Walters, the batting coach, was a guru of modern "scientific" techniques—pull your top hand off the bat when you follow through; take your weight off your back foot; lean into the pitch; swing down on the ball.

One afternoon, the rookie and minor league pitchers were herded to the batting cage by Chuck and Norm Simon, the bench coach, who handed out helmets and bats. Norm announced, "The New York Diamonds are a team in the Eastern Division of the Senior Circuit. Our league plays baseball the old fashioned way, which means the pitcher comes up to bat. Every single one of you has to take batting practice."

Willy was a decent softball hitter, but her timing and quickness in wielding a bat had grown rusty and dull. Indeed, she was not dissimilar from most of the other pitchers in that regard. Most of these guys had never even used a wooden bat before turning pro, but Papp made her practice with the real thing, a genuine Louisville Betsy. Nonetheless, she was particularly awkward and her cohorts gave her a royal razzing.

"Whoa! Henrietta Aaron! Look out! My, oh, my, it's Regina Jackson! The daughter of the Sultan of Swat she is not!"

"Can I bunt, Chuck?" she pleaded.

"That's tomorrow's clinic," answered the batting coach. There was a collective groan from the minor league twirlers.

The veteran Diamonds in camp were acutely concerned with the preseason tone of the New York sportswriters' ink spots about the team and its players as they played themselves into shape. Willy, like the other rookies and farmhands, knew the wags were around, but she was totally unaware of what Dale Goodwyn wrote in the *Daily Mail*: "Besides the two newest of the star-spangled Diamonds, Jacobson and Fortune, the most talked about items in Diamond Town are The Girl (that's a new twist) and The Eye Opener (there's one of these every spring), the hot pitching prospect who unexpectedly dazzles the manager and coaching staff. The Eye Opener and The Girl are both named Willy Beal."

As she waited for her daily pitching workout with Rudy and Shanks, Willy sat to rest on the ground and shared a can of no-caff cola with one of her peers, Jay Phillips. Willy chatted with Jay while she leaned forward to scrutinize the crowd of reporters, fans, and kids hanging and climbing on the outside of the fence, several rows deep and solidly lining the perimeter of the practice field. "Is it always like this?" Willy asked.

Jay laughed in disbelief. "Are you completely clueless? It's you they've come to see." Willy's eyes widened as she surveyed the elder gents staring, the confounded looking middle-aged men, the ladies occasionally shaking their heads, but more often nodding, the middle-aged and younger women, yuppies and soccer moms along with their kids, all yelling, whistling, pointing, and clapping. Every time Willy walked by, bent over, threw a ball, caught a ball, or tied her shoes the crowd stirred.

Shanks and Rudy—already hauled on the carpet by Tom for spending a disproportionate amount of time with one particular young pitcher—stood together watching Willy's methodically fluid motion. Said Rudy Judd, "That wrist snapping is how she gets the slider to break and it puts the kick in her fastball."

"She's got big league stamina," said Shanks.

"She just might make it, Lew."

Shanks sniffled. "It ain't even a question. She's wet behind the ears. We gotta see how she does with real, live competition."

"She'll come around. Give her time, Lew."

Lew Shankleton laughed loudly, "Ha! We ain't on no five-year plan here, ya know."

"Aw, no," despaired Rudy. "We're not gonna rush her, are we? We'll ruin that beautiful arm."

"She's tough, Rudy," Shanks said. "She'll be yours and Tom's before September."

Both Shanks and Rudy called Willy *honey, dear, sweetie,* and *sweetheart,* terms which, indicative of endearment or not, would have sparked a rebuke from Willy in another place, another time. Here and now, however, their expressions were so genuinely innocent—quite like the way they referred to the other pitchers as "son"—that she easily accepted and returned their warmth and fondness. Her workout finished, Willy looked over at the two wise men talking–probably arguing–about the way Jay planted his left foot after releasing a pitch. She could hardly wait for tomorrow to come. Throwing for Rudy and Shanks was almost like being in the backyard with Papp again. She bit her lip and closed her eyes to see her grandfather's face, grinning and saying with a wink, "Listen to 'em, li'l gal. They're both good men. You can learn a lot from 'em." Willy stood on the shoulders of a giant. Now she glimpsed the stars and heaven was within her grasp, but Rube was gone. *Why couldn't he have lived long enough to see this day?* Willy felt at once a warm glow and a dreadful ache in her breast. She walked to the farthest corner of the practice field and seated herself on the ground, not in the lotus position, but closed, with her arms and legs drawn up, like a tulip. She remained still and covered her face with her hands until she was all cried out.

Chapter 11

On the second weekend of spring training, Sebastian Fabian breezed into camp, followed by a mob of "his people," to announce the signing of Demeter Fortune to a multiyear contract. Demmy would later tell Cal, "Fabian walks over to me and says, 'Let's do the deal. How much and how long?' So, I told him and he says, 'It's done.' That was it!"

A blonde woman wearing a white golfing visor and sunshades was glued to Fabian's side. She stood erectly and her mouth never moved to speak.

"Is that his wife?" Willy asked Zinger.

"If it is," he laughed, "she's not the same one he had last season."

A reporter asked Fabian why he became personally involved in the negotiation of Fortune's contract and if it signaled a more active role as owner. Fabian snapped, "I paid ninety million dollars for this franchise. I could sell it today for half a billion. We're one of only five teams that'll take in two hundred million dollars in revenue. We have a hundred million dollar payroll. We have a broadcast and cable contract worth fifty million. Of course I'm involved. If I weren't, I'd be a fool. Come to think of it, that was a dumb question."

When Fabian cited the fifty million dollar broadcasting package, someone muttered, "That must've been one tough negotiation, since he owns the team and the sports channel." Willy watched Sebastian Fabian, his face familiar from the covers of scandal rags as well as business and sports magazines. He greeted the players and made small talk. Everyone addressed him as Mister Fabian, which, for all but the greenest of rookies, was more sarcastic than deferential.

Fabian was especially solicitous to Cal and Gil, both of whom he obviously held in high regard. Willy was tongue-tied and nervous when she met the jet-set celebrity. She was self-conscious about her damp palms, but Fabian's innocuous salutation of "Welcome!" was conveyed with an almost seductive quality, as he wrapped his hands around hers and smiled warmly. "Spectacular eyes!" he said to the woman clinging to his arm as they walked away. "She stands out, even in a crowd of stars."

Shortly afterward, Harvey Wanamaker, who had yet to introduce himself to Willy, jostled her and barked, "Beal, Greene, Strickland, Phillips, and Zanetsky come to Vallery's office. Mister Fabian wants you to sign your personal service contracts." Personal service covered appearances, endorsements, and publicity work on behalf of the team and paid fifty thousand dollars, which bonus baby Darnell called "chump change." Harvey said, "We want to get players signed up before they make the Diamonds. It kicks in if and when you're called up." The Diamonds' preseason exhibition games would begin the following Wednesday. Today's business was batting practice with a multimedia menagerie of wags in attendance. Willy was one of the minor leaguers brought over to the big league side of the complex to toss the horsehide to the slugging Diamonds. To be selected to throw bee-pee was akin to being chosen for bloody martyrdom in a game called: "Let's drub the scrub."

"This ain't a tryout," Shanks said to Willy, as he led her onto the Diamond Town field's artificial turf. "So don't try to get cute."

Afterward, Demeter Fortune went into the batting cage to take a few swings against Iron Mike, the pitching machine. Cal Bonham yelled, "Hey, six-for-one's taking some bee-pee!" He was ribbing Fortune about being traded for six players, although he had been swapped for five just a year ago. Cal clenched the steel weave of the cage with both arms outstretched. He stuck his feet into the mesh and swung from side to side with acrobatic agility as a few other players meandered over to watch. Cal called through the steel curtain, "Let's have a look at Fortune." Demmy spewed sunflower seeds on the ground and settled into his left-handed stance. Pronounced Cal, "He's got the right name, doesn't he?" Demmy flicked off the first serve from Iron Mike. "Ah-ha! Six-for-one's money belt's slowing him down." Demmy swung down on the next one from Iron Mike and sent it straight into the dirt, about two feet in front of him. He glared at Cal and turned around to swing right-handed. "Uh-oh! Now he's going to try it the other way." Demmy smacked the next offering in the general direction of the sun. "Learn anything yet?" he shouted to Cal.

"Maybe!"

"Want to see what I learned from you, Bonham?"

"Yeah!"

Demmy turned back around to the left side, went down on his knees, choked up on the bat more than halfway to the barrel, and screamed in a high-pitched falsetto, "Now batting, number twelve, Calvin Bonham, second base!" Then Demeter Fortune threw the bat at Iron Mike's next pitch.

Cal jumped down from the cage, laughing gleefully. "I never throw the bat!" he said.

Willy found Zinger yakking with a group of players. "Ditch the inflatable Buffy Bimbo doll," he said. "Here comes the girl." Zinger would sometimes sneak up from behind and tickle Willy with a bat. Sometimes she would creep up when his back was turned and gently clunk him on the head with a ball. Their silliness was imbued with playful joy. Zinger was a pal.

Zinger's wife, Michelle, was in Florida for the week and Willy joined them for a bite to eat at the Diamond Town deli. Steve and Michelle Filsinger chewed pastrami and corned beef sandwiches, slurped coffee, argued, chain-smoked cigarettes, and told funny stories about their two kids, Stephanie and Mikey. She loved Michelle as much as Zinger.

Willy met several other spouses as well, including Cal's ex-wife, Cleo, who came by with their son, Eugene. She was "drop-dead gorgeous" and intelligent, and her relationship with Cal seemed cordially civilized. Willy wondered why they couldn't make it. While Zinger and Michelle were a pair of mismatched sizes—she was tiny and petite in contrast to her burly hubby—Leota Douglas was very nearly a female version of Big Gil, a handsome, powerful athlete. Lizann Burton was in Florida, but sight unseen, and Lorraine Cello remained home in New Jersey. Paul spent the fall and winter playing house-husband, his wife apparently taking to her bed after birthing their third daughter. "Lorraine just didn't bounce back like her old self this time," said Paul.

"Pregnancy and childbirth isn't a disease, Paul," Zinger

grated unsympathetically.

"It's natural, but it's not normal, Zinger," Paul stated.

Willy also met Andy Gilbert's Amerasian wife, Kwan Lin, who carried herself with poise, but spoke in a frail, quivering voice. Leave it to Psycho Bielski to say, "You'd expect Andy to hook up with Peggy Sue from Brushy Mountain, but he goes and nails Suzie Wong from Hong Kong."

"She's Thai, Psycho," Willy said with annoyance.

"Thai? Same difference!" insisted the Psycho, adding, "She's got cute little bazoomies, though."

"Shush!" Willy shouted, reaching to grab his hand to spank it. "Shame on you!"

"What'd I say?" Then he added impishly, "If you're one of us, one of the guys, you gotta let us talk like guys, girlfriend."

There was a workout in the morning before Tuesday afternoon's intrasquad game. Ten minor leaguers, including Willy, were invited to take part along with the forty Diamonds on the official roster. The workout would be serious and closed to the public, but the game was a contrived media event to which the Diamonds sold tickets.

Cal Bonham deliberately targeted Demeter Fortune for continued ribbing and half-serious challenges "to keep him loose and to get tight with him at the same time." Hence, during the morning workout, Cal hailed for all to hear, "Where's the fastest white guy on the team?"

"Fastest *white* guy?" cried Demmy. "I'm the fastest *guy* on the team."

"Just what I hoped you'd say, six-for-one. Let's get to it." Cal and Demmy attracted the attention of their teammates as they marched toward home plate. "The most important ninety feet in all of baseball." Cal pointed to first base.

"Spoken like a true banjo singles hitter," Demmy replied.

"Hey," yelled Cal. "Somebody come here and watch so this guy doesn't cheat."

"And somebody go to first to make sure the midget doesn't try to trip me."

They crouched on either side of the white line, each with his left leg tucked under his chin and right foot touching back on the plate. Joe Manlius, hovering over the second baseman and the shortstop, said something sufficiently funny or obscene to trigger them to giggle as they raised their trunks high in the air. Joe called, "On your marks, get set, bang!"

Fifty major and minor league players and coaches screamed, shouted, jumped, and clapped while the two men streaked alongside each other. Nobody thought to get a stopwatch, but Willy counted, "One Mississippi, two Mississippi . . . " and never reached four, as Fortune's toe hit the base half a stride ahead of Bonham's.

"Okay," said Cal, between puffing breaths. "Banjo hitter, huh? Let's do some steals and extra bases and tagging up all at once. The whole three-sixty!"

"You're on, slow bro'!"

"Aw, you're dead meat now, six-for-one."

The assembled Diamonds put down bets for beers, a few bucks, and "my wife against yours," as the two returned to their starting positions.

Joe barked, "No cuttin' on the base paths. Cal, stay on the inside of the bag. Demmy, stay on the outside. Got that?" They both nodded without a trace of good humor. Again, Joe hollered the word "bang" and they were off. This time, turning at first, rather than running past the base, Cal made up the half step and led the way toward second, where Demmy came and stayed astride until they rounded third. Cal blatantly cut the corner. Demmy took a wide, out-of-path turn, as one would do in a game, but still poured on enough of a final spurt to hit the plate sliding, well ahead of Cal. Walking with hands on hips and huffing heavily as Demmy bent over to catch his breath, Cal announced, "Out of my class! No fair! I'm over thirty. We need a real test before we hand you the crown. We need a kid."

Demmy straightened himself, spat on the turf, and said, "Bring him on!"

"Wil-lee! Oh, Wil-lee!" Cal's tenor voice lilted.

Willy, wearing her hair pulled back in a bun today, looked directly down at her feet, shaking her head. Cal kept calling her until someone from behind ignited a bullish chant of "Wil-lee, Wil-lee, Wil-lee!" She walked forward, head still tilted downward, but eyes now peering at Bonham and Fortune. "Oh, all right," she said slowly, deliberately, and calmly, as her pulse throbbed in her throat and the adrenaline began to surge.

"You better take five first," suggested Willy. "Have some water or Alligade." Demmy shook his head. "I wanna beat you, not kill you!" she laughed, almost but not quite tauntingly.

He shook his head again. "No! Let's go now!"

Fortune's blue eyes were ablaze and his smile turned into a scowl as Willy snapped, "Suit yourself, Demmy!"

Joe, obviously relishing the role of field judge, shouted instructions: "Start together, stay even with the left side batter's box, towards the home team dugout, then out to the warnin' track. Stay on the warnin' track, and come down in front of the visitors' dugout before cuttin' in to cross the plate. Ya gotta touch the plate," said Joe, who lost his smile upon seeing that the man and the woman were locked in a cold stare.

"Boy rabbit versus girl rabbit," came a quip. After Willy

opened a lead of three full strides passing first, Demmy gradually closed the gap and came abreast of her as they passed the right field corner. Four times, Willy pulled ahead only to have Demmy catch up a few seconds later, finally moving in front as they crossed the left field foul line. "She's gonna run outta gas if she tries to sprint ahead of him another time."

Willy remained one step behind Demmy until she sensed him quickening to shift gears for the final stretch when they motored past third, approaching the far side of the visitors' dugout. "Here comes the double-clutch. She's history."

Willy yelled, "Bye-bye!" and exploded away from Demeter Fortune like a retro-fired satellite separating from its booster rocket. "Sonofagun!" She touched home plate at full speed and didn't slow down by so much as a step before she raised her arms in the air in front of the home dugout. Demmy, hopelessly vanquished, had slowed to a walk by the time he reached the plate, where he planted his butt to receive the jeers of his mates. Emerging victorious from her pseudo-manhood ritual of fire, Willy waded through the back-slapping accolades of her fellow farmhands and Diamonds, and approached her downtrodden foe. "You're still the fastest *guy* on the team, Demmy." Willy felt a tremor of regret and emptiness when Paul Cello wrapped his arm around her waist.

"If you're finished showin' off for the menfolk, we got work to do." She gave him a questioning look, trying not to let on that she thrilled at his touch. "Tom wants ya to work a couple innings in the intrasquad game," Paul said. "Just listen to me, babe. I'll take good care of ya."

Willy pitched two innings in the intrasquad game, yielding two hits between two ground outs and a strikeout in the fifth.

Paul came out to talk to her after each play, telling her how to pitch to the next batter, slapping her rump, even rubbing her neck. He was pure bedrock. Then all hell broke loose with wild cheering from both benches when she punched out the side in the sixth, although the only real Diamond she fanned was Thor Andreason, a lefty, crossed up by Willy's backdoor slider.

After the game concluded, Dale Goodwyn asked Darnell, one of Willy's strikeout victims, how she looked to him. "She was lookin' good," he told the reporter. "Real good! First time I ever whiffed with a hard-on, man." All manner of people managed to make their way inside the complex to gawk at and mingle with the players. A round-faced young man with tousled brown hair came up to Willy carrying a briefcase and digital camera. "No interviews!" she said to him, raising her palm to signal halt.

He chattered nervously, "I'm from the Great American Baseball Card and Bubble Gum Company. Can you spare a minute to look over our standard contract? After you sign it, we can take some pictures." He produced a document for Willy to read while she sat cross-legged on the ground. He sighed and planted his butt next to hers after a moment. "The contract's the same for everybody. The big stars don't get more out of it unless we do a special series. We have basic contracts with Big League Baseball, Inc. and the players' union and we try to have all players signed up with us when they're still in the minors." Willy looked at him, doffed her cap, and said, "Where do I sign?" Willy scrawled her name. "My picture on a baseball card!" Willy threw back her head and laughed mightily. *The little girl inside peeked out to see herself wearing a grown-up big leaguer's uniform. Awesome!*

Upon returning to the Halladay Inn for a supper of yogurt,

bananas, and strawberries, Willy phoned Alma in Saint Pete. "You had a long-distance call from Canada, Willy Mae," said Alma, "from a very charming young lady named Amy Jones. Amos's grandchild? So articulate! She wanted to tell you herself that her mother gave birth to an eight-pound, six-ounce baby girl. She's called Caitlin Louise. Then she said, 'now there are three soul mates.' She said you'd know what that means."

Willy, sobbing happily, dialed Toronto after hanging up from Mama and spoke with both Amy and Katie. There was more good news. James had latched onto a job managing an independent team in Oregon. "But their season doesn't start 'til June," complained Kate. "His spring training job ends the first week of April. Then he's at home for two months, getting in my hair. It'll be like having *five* kids."

After talking to Katie, Willy thought about Peter and the guys with the Buffalo Wolves in Orlando. She wanted to get away to visit them but knew she was unlikely to find the time and there were no games between the Wolves and Diamonds on the exhibition schedule.

After a week of barnstorming by bus through the Citrus Circuit, the Diamonds returned to Deerfield Beach for a weekend home stand against their intracity rivals from Old New York. "Crosstown warfare, ya know what I'm sayin'?" the Reb explained. "Even last year . . . we were in the thick of it and they were in the toilet . . . but the yahoos come from Queens to see the Amazin' Ones or from the Bronx to see the Bombers in Jersey . . . like we were the visitors in our own park."

"I think things will be different this season," Willy offered.

"Believe it, cuz," Sandy Lee said definitively.

Larry and Sandy Lee wondered as they walked nearby the

other team's dugout whether Willy couldn't hear or simply ignored the verbal darts chucked her way. "I do believe she signed her contract with them long legs open wide for the owner man! . . . I could handle some of that sweet thang! . . . Like you can't tell a lesbo when you see one? . . . Ha-haa!" Unbeknownst to Willy, Sandy Lee would pay a visit to the other team's dugout with a promise to bust some heads if they kept up their off-color harassment of his female teammate.

Willy would sit idly in the Diamond bullpen on Saturday and Sunday. Despite the stellar status of Brooks and Langevin, Zinger ruled the bullpen. He led the over-the-fence banter with the spectators, decided whether to throw back or puncture runaway beach balls, and told the Kiddie Korps pitchers, including Willy, riding the wooden bench, when to turn their rally caps inside out. Willy hated to be a player in practice sessions and a nonplayer in the exhibition games. She also began to fret about being let go at the end of spring training. A few days passed before she mustered the nerve to confront Tom Vallery.

"Am I just here to make Fabian and the Diamonds look good for inviting a woman to spring training?"

Tom was surprised and amused. "It's complicated, Willy. You're a special case . . . "

"I don't wanna be treated special!" she said, cutting him off.

"I agree," Tom sighed. "It's not fair to you. The media's itching to see you. Whatever you do will be blown out of proportion . . . if you blow 'em away . . . if you get knocked around."

"Just one inning, one batter . . . please!" she implored, jiggling theatrically.

"Be patient, Willy," Tom said coolly. "Paul, Rudy, and Shanks are very high on you. They don't give that kind of praise lightly. I like what I've seen, too. You'll get your chance."

Two days later, Diamond Town was stood on its proverbial ear–perhaps as a portent of things to come–when three lefties, Bruce Jacobson, rookie Jay Phillips, and reliever Tim Langevin, combined for a no-hit, no-run, no-flaws perfect game, leading to some decidedly premature pennant fever. Paul backstopped all nine innings of *el perfecto*. He was then set upon by a battery of wags. "Absolutely meaningless," he disclaimed. "An exhibition game! Don't even count! I was in on a real gem with Sandy Lee two years back. That was nice. This is nothin'!"

The cameras scoped out the insufferable Bruce Jacobson. He delivered sound bites and non-sequiturs in seriously measured clichés. "I felt loose . . . I had my good stuff . . . I put the ball where I wanted it . . . I stayed within myself . . . " Jake's was the arm of the hour and he wrapped himself in ribbons for the media and fandom up in Gotham City.

A visiting celebrity of sorts made the rounds the next day. Elliot Birdsong, a former big leaguer, still only in his thirties, attracted calls of "long time, no see" from several players. Birdsong was fit, trim, handsome, and downright charming. Willy called him "Mr. Smooth." Birdsong had made a name for himself at the all-star game a few years back with an inside-the-park home run and a pair of stolen bases. Then, he was traded, faded, and gone.

"I guess I was washed up young," he ventured easily. "I stay close to the game. I know a lot of players, personally and professionally. My consultancy business is doing good things for my clients."

"Uh-oh, I get it," Willy said with her enchanting laugh. "You wanna be my agent, right?"

"I'll be your valentine, too!" he said, flashing his winning smile.

"Forget that!"

"Let's talk some business then," he suggested. "Dinner?"

In recent days, she had rebuffed invitations from Larry, who was married, and Darnell, who was not, since they seemed to suggest something more than teammates hanging together for an evening. She honestly felt guilty about socializing with an outsider, so wrapped up was she in the cocoon of Diamond Town.

"We could go to my friend's crib. He's got a condo nearby. He's having some people over to party. There'll be a couple of Diamonds there and players from other teams, too."

"Forget about dinner, Elliot. I'm a serious working girl. I need my rest and meditation, but we can visit your friend for a little while and talk business."

Willy wore a frilly pink blouse, stretchy slacks, not her holey jeans, and her going-out shoes, but she couldn't outshine the bodacious Birdsong, with his sporty XYZ car, high-ticket Swiss watch, and his big-name designer jacket. Willy's imagination was working overtime, sensing that her chums on the team were whispering about her rendezvous with Mr. Smooth. The condominium complex where Birdsong's friend resided had one of those ostentatious names like Imperial Gardens or Estates or Arms. On the car ride, not surprisingly, he didn't discuss one iota of business. Outside, as they walked from his car, Mr. Smooth's hands, promptly smacked away, probed Willy's shoulders, waist, and hips. Willy despaired that Birdie didn't seem to understand the difference between a potential client and a potential booty call. Elliot tapped at the door, which vibrated with music, talking, and laughter from within. The door opened and Elliot's friend, whom he called D.W., welcomed them. The room was dimly lit, but noisy, and the air was thickly hazed. A remix of the Spinners' cover of the Four Seasons' classic boomed, *"Workin' my way back to you, babe . . . "* The smell of burnt rope singed Willy's nostrils.

"The smokin' lamp is lit, I guess you could say," was what D.W. said.

Panning the room and a dozen strangers' faces, Willy's eyes met those of Darnell Greene, poised with a straw over a glass tabletop, ready to snort a line of white powder. *Coke fried rookie!* She winced and turned away in disgust.

"I gotta go!" she hissed to Elliot as she retreated for the still open door.

"Come on, be cool, baby . . . " he said softly.

"Don't call me baby!" she snapped. Elliot reached for Willy's arm and she slapped his hand.

"You crazy or what?"

"Maybe," she said with a derisive laugh, "but now I know why your career went down the tubes so fast."

"Oh, give me a break!" he moaned. "I had a torn Achilles' tendon, four knee operations in five years, and a detached retina. I could've been blind."

"You're blind, all right," sneered Willy, as she once again turned for the door. Birdsong stood in the doorway, deflated and no longer charming. Willy's anger turned to pity, even sadness for him. The poor fool really didn't understand, she thought, but he wasn't her problem.

"Can't I at least drive you back to your motel?"

"Willy can walk!" she sang almost cheerfully, skipped

down the steps, swung her carryall bag by its straps, and slipped off her going-out shoes. "In fact, Willy runs!" she called back to him, and sprinted away in her bare feet. In a fortunate throwback to her earlier life of jogging to and from work at the high school in Saint Pete, Willy always kept a pair of sneakers in her carryall out of habit. She sat in the dewy grass in front of the condos to put on her sneaks, and began to sing aloud for no one but herself to hear. Figuring that she was still a good five miles from the Halladay Inn, Willy instead set out for Diamond Town, an easy two-mile sprint. She hung the carryall bag behind her neck, weaving the strap under her arms and over her shoulders, so that it clapped against her back at rhythmic two-stride intervals. A cool breeze in the nighttime air sent a flutter through Willy's blouse and she felt a refreshing chill against the sweat on her neck, face, and shoulders.

When Willy reached the main gate of the spring training complex, her eyes caught Paul Cello, squatting in front of a floodlight in the parking lot. "Fancy meeting you here!" she called, as he greeted her with a quick flip of his hand.

"I thought ya were out on the town with Pretty Boy Birdsong."

Willy told Paul what happened and he shook his head. "Somebody should've said somethin' to ya. Zinger wanted to go tell ya Birdsong was bad news, but Cal said ya were a big girl, that ya can take care of yourself. I didn't wanna stick my nose in, but . . . "

Willy smiled, but shook her head. "Cal's right," she said sternly. "I'm not exactly a child, you know." Willy hunkered down next to Paul on the hard pavement. He sat cross-legged, she sat in the lotus, and their knees touched. "What are you doing camped out here in the parking lot?"

"Waitin' for the pizza man," the catcher said, pretending to look at an imaginary timepiece on his unadorned wrist. "They promise to deliver in fifteen minutes, or else it's a freebie."

A dilapidated compact car buzzing around the lot turned out to be the pizza man. Paul handed the driver a fistful of bills and took the flat, white box, laying it on the ground. "Want some?" he asked her.

"What kind is it?"

"Pepperoni," he said, opening the box and cautiously separating the pieces to cool.

"Forget about it!" she hooted. "Haven't you noticed I'm like 'no meat, no way'?"

"So, you're a complete and total vegetarian?" he asked, picking off a slice of pepperoni and munching it.

"I tried being a vegan a few years ago . . ." she started to say.

"A what, a Vulcan?" Paul kidded.

"A vegan!" she laughed, digging her knuckles into his shoulder. "A nondairy vegetarian, no animal products at all, but I found out I crave cheese. I like yogurt, too. So, I'm a lacto-ovo vegetarian, which means I eat eggs and drink milk, but only organic."

"I'm a junk food junkie, sorry to say." Paul also had no problem talking with his mouth full of cheesy pizza. "The baby, Meredith, is allergic to breast milk. Talk about traumatic! For Lorraine, that is. Megan was a good baby, slept through the night. Ashley was somethin' else! She'd wake up, nurse, still be hungry, gulp a whole bottle of formula, and then stay awake cryin'. Since she was like four days old, I'd lay her on top of me and she'd fall asleep suckin' on my nose. Isn't that wild? She still sucks her fingers. She's six now."

Willy suddenly slapped her shoulder and gave it a quick rub. "Skeeters are out early," she said, then wrapped her arms across her chest, hugging herself in the same manner Peter Jones observed months before.

Paul told Willy his story. "Catchin' is supposed to be the fastest track to the majors, but I stayed six years in the minors. I never batted under .300 and I hit sixteen homers in Triple-A. Sometimes just bein' good ain't good enough. Frisco called me up in September and I went to spring trainin' thinkin' I was their regular catcher. It was a lock! Then, along comes Gary Steele before the season starts. He got into a contract squabble with Washington and demanded to be traded. So, Frisco gets him and I'm carryin' his jockstrap. I'm playin' maybe two games a month, not even once a week, like most backups, and catchin' warm-ups in the pen. It was the pits! Luckily, Tom Vallery was managin' in Chicago and he needed a backup and they bought my contract. When Tom came to New York, he brought me, Zinger, Benny, and Thor along with him. The Diamonds liked me 'cause I came cheap. A month into the season, Jeff McCarty gets hurt and I'm number one. Eight years and countin'!" Paul momentarily ceased his monologue, charmed by the way Willy listened so intently. "Melted any rocks with those eyes lately?" he teased with a grin. Willy blinked and turned her head away, embarrassed. "I'm sorry," he said in a voice that was deeper, softer, before rising in pitch to add, "I'm the most married guy in the world, but I'm not the only one who's taken quite a shine to ya. You're a complicated package, babe."

She beamed and leaned to rest her chin on her drawn-up knees. "What do you think about the pitching part of the package, Paul?"

"I think you, Phillips, and Zanetsky are the most advanced minor league pitchers in camp. Right now we got the best front three in baseball, but, in a year or two, we could have four twenty-game winners . . . and the fourth ace won't be either of those guys."

"You think I'm good, huh?" she asked with deliberate coyness.

"I think you're a big question mark. It's not ability you lack, but experience. You've got the natural talent. You've got baseball brains, too, but I've seen lots of good pitchers who didn't make it. Lots of things can happen . . . injuries, tendinitis—the silent killer!" He raised his hands, clawing with his fingers. Paul noticed that Willy was once again rapt with interest, a slight but anxious smile on her parted lips.

"Are you gonna be my teacher, Paul?"

"I'll try," he said with a reassuring wink.

The floodlights cast enough of a glow to reflect Willy's enticing smile and the sparkling luminance of her eyes. "I want you to teach me," she said, at once innocently and proudly, observed Paul.

Something is happening here, Willy thought to herself. She wasn't listening to his words, but the timbre of his voice. She wasn't looking at his face, but dancing with his eyes. *Everything on the outside says no, Willy. But on the inside . . . where are these feelings coming from? I think I'm gonna explode. If he so much as touches me . . .*

The two sets of brown eyes met once more. On the verge of losing all sense of time, place, and purpose, Willy sighed and offered a change of pace. *I've gotta put up an invisible wall.* "Tell me some more stories about Lorraine and the girls." *It worked! I found the safety zone.*

Willy enjoyed the immediate, delightful transformation of

the Diamonds' catcher to happy daddy, relating how, when Ashley was only three, she had asked him, "If we died and went to heaven and our car was in the driveway, would people think we were home?"

Willy was too tired to jaunt another few miles and consented to Paul's offer of a ride back to the motel. She slept as if in a coma. By the time she arrived at Diamond Town for the morning workout, she had come to terms with events of the night before, but she saw Darnell Greene and flushed with anger. Psycho Adam Bielski told Max, "She was in Darnell's face all mornin'. She's always kissin' up to Cal, Zinger, and Sandy Lee. Them guys drink. Don't try and tell me they never smoked no weed. Larry Brooks ain't even sober one day at a time. I can't figure her out, man."

Max smiled knowingly. "Ain't nothin' to figure out, Psycho. Willy's got values. Know what values are?"

Chapter 12

On Monday, Willy got the word from Shanks that she had despaired about for weeks. "We're playin' split-squad games against Minnesota today. Tom and Rudy want ya to work an innin' against the Twinkies' scrubeenies in the B-squad game up in Fort Myers." Shanks yelled "Jeez!" as Willy squeezed and kissed him.

Coach Norm Simon managed the Diamond B team in the game and Paul worked behind the plate to give Tom a first-hand report on five youngsters, including Willy, slated to share nine innings of pitching under fire. During the two-hour ride on the team bus a deep, hollow pain in the pit of Willy's stomach formed, making her irrationally wish that Norm would forget to put her in the game. On the bench in the visiting team's dugout, Willy entertained Max and Psycho by folding and unfolding her hands, jiggling her knees, rubbing her nose, taking her cap off, putting it back on, then removing it again, and scrunching it up.

"What's the matter with ya?" asked the Psycho with a shout.

"What the heck ya think's the matter with her?" interjected

Paul. "She's nervous, ya twit!"

"Nervous, you say?" Willy looked up, still jiggling. "More like scared! Look at this!" She snapped her fingers against the ligature NY inside the gold-colored diamond-shaped emblem on the dark blue cap, slapped the skyline logo arm patch, ran her finger down the red, white, and blue trouser stripes, and pinched the fabric of her on-the-road jersey with "New York" written in script on the front. "I've been playin' make-believe for a month, but today it's for real!"

Between the fifth and sixth innings, Norm told Willy to warm up and a few minutes later she scampered to the pitcher's mound. There were less than a thousand onlookers on hand, the real game between the Minnesotans and the Diamonds being in Deerfield Beach, but no one could recall a more enthusiastic reception for a visiting team's player in Fort Meyers. Yet Willy didn't notice anything. She muddled through half a dozen practice tosses to Paul and watched the first of the Minnie B team's scrubs strut to the plate to bat. She tried to concentrate, but her arm felt limp and she was sweating buckets. She pitched a curve up and in, a fastball down and away, a fastball up and in, and a curve down and away. The Minnie rook took a walk to first base. Paul made no move to talk to his pitcher, but his return throws came back to her harder and quicker between pitches as she missed the inside corner with a backdoor slider and missed the outside corner with a breakaway slider to the next hitter. Ball three was a sidearm fastball that went over the batter's head and nearly glided past Paul's mitt to the screen. Ball four was an overhand curveball that bounced on the plate. That brought Paul out to have a word with Willy. He threw back his catcher's mask, spit on the ground, and screamed so close to her face that his chest pushed against hers. "You're spottin' the freakin' ball. Enough with the nerves already! Darn it all, Willy! These clowns aren't even as good as the guys ya murdered in winter ball. They suck!" Willy backed up, averted her eyes, and drew lazy circles in the dirt with the toe of her cleats. "Are ya ticked off at me?" Paul barked.

"Yeah!" she responded without casting an eye upon him.

"Good! Take it out on them," he said and turned away. The third batter tried to check his swing on a jumping sidearm fastball and knocked into a double play, putting a runner on third with two outs. After taking a called strike on a buggywhip fastball, the next Twinner chipped a slider on the ground to short and was easily tossed out at first, thankfully bringing Willy's one dreadful inning to a close.

"Smooth, baby," Paul teased sarcastically. "Really smooth!" Then he swatted Willy's butt and she got the glad hand from Norm, slapped fives with her mates, kicked back on the bench, popped a no-caff diet cola, and watched the rest of the game in good spirits. Paul had driven by car to Fort Myers and he coaxed her into riding back to Deerfield Beach with him after the game instead of busing it with the other players. "We can grab some eats and shoot the breeze, okay?"

Willy deliberately headed in the direction of some people standing behind a barrier, lingering at the gate to look at her, rather than moving on to the parking lot. "I can't keep avoiding them," she said to Paul. Willy was smiling and outwardly composed, but all aflutter inside as she neared the mostly female group. She felt a rush of emotion and energy as she heard one faceless woman say, "She's coming over!"

A dozen light, dark, stubby, chubby, ringed, naked, long, and thin fingers were reaching out to Willy as she offered her hand and said, "Hi, I'm Willy." Felt-tipped pens, Diamonds' yearbooks, and score sheets were passed into her hands and quickly snatched back after she bestowed her signature.

"Where are you from? . . . I grew up right here in Florida . . . From Canada? I have friends in Toronto. On vacation, right? . . . How old are you, honey? Twelve? I'm twenty-eight . . . Oops! Oh, I ripped the paper. Sorry about that! . . . I never even signed an autograph until this year . . . You're from where? . . . "

Amid the frenzy Willy was handed an old-fashioned book, with an off-white vinyl cover and collated yellow, pink, and blue pages. The uncapped, silver, engraved pen was carefully placed between Willy's fingers by an unsmiling fiftyish woman, who said, "You're a hero, Willy Beal. The first woman in Big League Baseball!"

"Not quite yet," Willy chuckled. "I haven't even played in the minors yet."

"You'll make it. You'll be great. I know it."

The woman suddenly lurched forward to kiss Willy's cheek. Startled, Willy just laughed and returned the pen and book. She next turned to a round face with blue eyes, framed by thin, curly, salt-and-pepper hair. This woman had a stern, dour look and stocky build, making Willy think of a prison guard, or maybe a particularly tough meter maid.

"I'm Lottie Richter," said the lady. "This is my husband, Karl." Karl smiled, showing noticeably ill-fitting dentures. He had thick, short, white hair and kindly eyes. "We're from Camden," Lottie said.

"New Jersey!" Willy said gleefully. "Hometown fans!"

"Oh, no, we hate New York! We root for Philly, but we'll come to cheer for ya if ya get to play in the City of Brotherly Love someday."

"Thank you," whispered Willy, as Lottie Richter firmly

gripped her hands with Willy's.

"When I was a young girl," said Lottie, "I could play sports just like the boys, even football. I loved to tackle! But baseball was what I loved best. Even after growin' up and gettin' married, I was the one who taught my sons to play sports. Karl's not much of an athlete." He smiled again, signaling agreement. "And my daughter, she played soccer and basketball in high school. I never thought about bein' a real baseball player. It just wasn't possible, no more than the man in the moon." Willy caught a glimmer of the young, healthy female athlete in Lottie's eyes. Lottie raised her large but smooth-skinned hands to Willy's face, gently cupping her cheeks. "Play out my dream for me, sweetheart."

Willy wrapped her arms around Lottie's broad shoulders and the two women hugged. Paul's voice wafted from afar. "What is goin' on?" They quickly parted as Paul reached for Willy's arm and whisked her away. "If you're finished!" he said mockingly. "Hey," he prodded, "ya shouldn't go around kissin' strange people, babe. Ya gotta keep your distance."

"You don't get it, Paul. Up until a couple of months ago, I was one of them." She added, "I still am." Less than five minutes after exiting the ballpark, Paul declared unbearable hunger. He lifted his foot from the gas pedal as the golden arches came into view—"No way, Paul!"—drove past them—"Don't play with me like that"—and pulled into the fast food competitor across the street. "Paul Cello! Why're you doing this to me?"

"C'mon, get a fishburger or chicken doodles or somethin'."

"Hush up! I'm mad at you," Willy said to Paul, but there was a happy bounce to her step as she walked through the door with him. Willy asked for a salad and a low-cal no-caff cola. She told the nattily uniformed matron at the register that most of America's protein was consumed by beef cattle and inefficiently passed on, second-hand, to human beings. The woman replied by asking, "Would you like a hot apple crispy with your order today?"

"Why do they call it fast food when ya gotta wait for ten minutes?" grumbled Paul, as he and Willy wordlessly looked at the man seated at the next table. His long grey hair, tinged yellow, flowed from beneath a soiled baseball cap bearing their very own New York D's insignia. He was sleeping deeply with his head buried in folded arms on the tabletop. "They're all over," said Paul. "They hang out in libraries, too. He'll probably eat from the dumpster after closing. It's really sad, isn't it?" Willy responded with a small smile that was both curious and pleased. "Surprised?" he sang. "Some of us dumb jocks are socially conscious . . . or not totally *un*conscious, anyways."

Willy whispered, "I know that."

Later in the day, back at Diamond Town, the locker room scuttlebutt on the minor league side was that Paul Cello was ripe for a young kid who could hit to come up and land a full-time job as the D's catcher. Psycho Bielski ridiculed the way pitchers spoke of "talking to Paul about the opposing hitters" as something akin to a religious ceremony, but Jay Phillips told Willy the coaches said Paul was "the manager's eyes and ears on the field."

"Besides, the best pitchers in the game say Cello's the best catcher in the game. That's good enough for me." Thus interjected a locker room visitor, who walked briskly toward the rookies, introduced himself as Art Ridzik, and extended his hand. Willy and Jay came away from his loaded handshake holding his business card, which read: *Arthur W. Ridzik,*

Attorney-at-Law, Sports & Entertainment Management.

Willy eyed him skeptically as she held up the card, twirling it between her fingers. "Send me your resume, and I'll get back to you." She spoke the brush-off deadpan, but his booming laugh and broad-faced smile elicited a grin in return.

"A man I used to know would've said to take a number and get in line," he said jovially.

"And who might that man be?" she asked.

Art looked at Willy, still smiling, and answered, "The plowboy from Georgia who knew every soul food kitchen and Italian restaurant in every major and minor league town in the US of A, and he took his pals to all of them."

For some reason Willy felt invaded or maybe under siege. "Oh, so you're trying to say you knew my grandfather?"

"That I did," he announced. "I worked my way through law school as a ballplayer, but, at the time, I thought I was working my way to the majors." He paused before continuing to speak more quietly, "I read his death notice in *The Baseball News*, but it was too late for the funeral. I felt bad about that. I sent a card. He was quite a man," Art said.

"Oh, yeah? Tell me about him," she challenged.

"I'm not after anything," he said. His eyes darted around the room for a moment, but he restored eye contact with Willy without hesitation. "I just want to meet Rube's pride and joy. Whether or not I can help you . . . professionally, I mean . . . is up to you."

"Let's go outside and talk, shall we?" Willy said in a pleasant, businesslike way. Art and Willy sat on the aluminum bleachers behind the practice field. "Where did you and Papp play together?"

"I was in the old Polo Grounders' farm system in the '50s. We were with the Jersey City Jerseys, Minneapolis Millers, and Dallas Eagles. We played in Phoenix, too. The parent clubs tried to duplicate the Manhattan-Brooklyn rivalry between Minneapolis and St. Paul and between Dallas and Ft. Worth."

"I know all of that," Willy said tersely. "Did you play for Mr. Leo?"

"No, Leo Durocher was long gone by the first time I got to go to spring training. Things were different then. All the kids from the farm teams didn't get invited to camp. I never made it to the Polo Grounds either, or . . . "

"Candlestick?" Willy suggested with a grin.

Art shook his head, heaved a labored sigh, and brought his face closer to hers. "The team played its first year out west at the old Seals Stadium. The 'Stick opened up in '60, as you know very well, I believe. Why're you trying to trip me up? I really did know Rube Henry."

Willy heard authenticity in Artie's storytelling and was now enjoying a visit with a newly found old-timer. "Who do you represent?" she asked.

"Well, no baseball players just yet," he answered, "but I've advised a number of high schoolers and negotiated their scholarship offers from colleges, and I work with lots of fellows my age, former athletes, to do personal appearances."

"I guess there's not much you can do for me. I signed a minor league contract and that's it until next season."

"If you have a good season, even another minor league contract for next year could be very lucrative. You've attracted a lot of attention already."

"Tell me about it!" said Willy, acting exasperated. "I'm beginning' to think my name is *her*. People say, 'Hey, that's *her*.' Other teams' players come to Diamond Town and say, 'Look, it's *her*.' It's getting to be kind of tired."

"That's why you need some guidance," he assured her. "And protection! Wait until people start to hit on you. Some famous athletes have been skinned alive by bad advice and poor business decisions."

"Ha! Business decisions?" laughed Willy, while clutching onto Artie's arm. "I don't even have a car of my own or a place to live yet."

"Let's say we have some dinner," said Artie. "We can talk business, if you want to, that is."

"What's the deal gonna be?" Willy asserted herself.

"My interest, you mean?" Art Ridzik pointed to himself and awaited her nod in response. "If we negotiate a new deal next year, I take four points. That's standard. On promotions, my fee is fifteen points. Some agents take twenty percent. Meantime, I'll work on publicity and endorsements. Being the first woman in Big League Baseball, you can write your own ticket, doing commercials and appearances . . . "

"You're kidding me! Commercials?"

"You're pretty enough to be a model . . . " Artie complimented unexpectedly.

Willy laughed, "Nobody ever said that until I started playing baseball."

"I can manage your money, finance that car and the living place you don't have yet, and set up your affairs so you can play baseball and forget about everything else. If I do any legal work for you, it's free." Willy didn't say anything. She suddenly felt weary. "We'll sign a contract between us." He assured her, "A straight business deal. I'll be working for you. I hope you trust me."

"I think I do," Willy replied, but she decided to call home later to ask Mama if Papp ever mentioned a man named Artie Ridzik.

"I'll meet you at the Diamond Town Cafe in half an hour," he said.

Willy agreed and went into the clubhouse. Shanks let her use his office phone to call Alma on her cell, then and there, rather than waiting.

"I certainly do know the name Art Ridzik. Papp said he encouraged him to go to law school because he didn't have a prayer as a baseball player," Alma told Willy, and the mother and daughter shared a laugh. "He wrote the kindest note when Papp passed away," Alma added.

At the cafe, Willy sipped a glass of spring water and watched Artie dine on a "cholesterol classic": bacon cheeseburger—oozing with blood, grease, and ketchup—steak fries, cole slaw, and onion rings. After he finished his feeding, Willy went back to the Halladay Inn with Artie Ridzik and signed a simple one-page contract, making him her agent.

When Willy got to Diamond Town the next day, she jived and clowned with her buddy, Zinger but began to feel a tinge of sadness. Spring training would close in a few days. Unless Willy was included in September's call-ups to collect splinters on the Diamonds' bench, which was probably a slim hope at best, she wouldn't see Zinger, Paul, Cal, Sandy Lee, or Big Gil for almost a year, until next spring.

At the end of the next-to-last week Willy received the news from Shanks about her regular season assignment. "We're sendin' ya to the Alexandria Dukes of the Mid-Atlantic League," he told her.

"Double-A?" Willy was breathing heavily, nearly hyperventilating.

"Yup." he said calmly.

"Not Single-A? Double-A!" she panted.

"That's what I said, isn't it?" As Willy nodded and fanned herself, he told her, "Ya get too excited, honey."

Hence began what is called "extended" training camp, where a hundred minor leaguers remained for another week of workouts, meetings, clinics, and simulated as well as intrasquad games. "Same old crap!" the Psycho said. Willy pitched two or three innings in each of five intrasquad games. Darnell and Max became almost laughably predictable strikeouts. Psycho, however, always managed to get a piece of the ball, although not necessarily for more than a bouncer or chopper. "Struck out by a girl! No balls at all, none of ya!" The ludicrousness of Bielski's razzing was actually refreshing, if not cathartic. As he said, "Darn, she's so good it's scary. Ain't it?"

Chapter 13

The most noteworthy event during the week of extended training camp was the Diamonds playing on opening day in Cincinnati.

The opener turned into a five-hour, seventeen-inning barnburner. Sandy Lee Danielson took the mound and was impressive in his debut, giving up four stingy hits, striking out five, and carrying a 1-0 lead into the ninth, but Larry Brooks came on and was tagged for a solo homer. Finally, mercifully, blessedly, Roy Burton found the pitch he wanted in his seventh time at bat and drilled it into the seats to win the game, 2-1.

By the time the Alexandria Dukes started their season the next week, the New York D's were 5-5, Sandy Lee and Big Gil had two wins apiece, Jake took two losses, and Zinger was drafted into the starting rotation. "Nobody's hurt bad enough to go on the disabled list yet," Psycho Bielski lamented.

Willy was nervous about finding an apartment in Alexandria, Virginia because the Dukes would barely touch base there for a few hours before beginning their Mid-Atlantic

League schedule with a road trip.

Dan Blanchard managed the Dukes. Willy felt a bit leery of Dan, vaguely sensing that he resented being the one who was stuck with *the girl* on his team. She approached him with dread when he asked her into his office during the team's quick stopover in Alexandria. Instead of addressing her from behind his desk, he joined her on the couch.

"I noticed how ya like to loosen up by yourself, then go shower and change before a game. Maybe ya should use my office."

"Are you worried about hanky panky in the showers, Dan?"

"No, I'm not worried 'bout ya!" he said with genuine certitude. "I just thought there might be times when ya want your privacy. Maybe on the days ya start a game. Well, my office is available."

Now at ease with Dan, Willy slid closer to him, tilted her head, and asked, "Hey, how did an old hardball head like you get to be so sensitive?"

Dan jerked his thumb and forefinger as if to count. "I got five sisters and four daughters . . . and I was smart enough to marry a woman smarter than me."

"That must be it," Willy said warmly as they sat side by side on the couch.

Aboard the bus to Wheeling, West Virginia, Willy borrowed Laddy Zanetsky's Swiss army knife to carve up slices of apple and banana, dipped them in peanut butter, and passed them among her teammates. "Weren't you actually born in Poland?" she asked Laddy.

"That's right," he replied with the slightest trace of an accent. "Laddy's short for Ladislaw." Both Jay and Laddy had a wife and small child living back home with parents or in-laws.

"What's the baby's name?" asked Willy.

"John Paul," answered Laddy with a hint of embarrassment.

"It means something special to you, doesn't it?" she said to him, gently touching the side of his neck from which hung a medallion showing the Crown of Saint Stephen.

"Do you have to know everything about everybody?" Todd Strickland asked teasingly. "Wanna see the tattoo on my butt?"

"Shush!" Willy told Strick.

John Pantagones was Alexandria's catcher. Perhaps because his teammates thought John resembled a character from a comic strip, or, since he spent a goodly amount of time digging the tosses of brain-dead heavers out of the dirt, all the Dukes called him Pigpen.

Dan picked Laddy to start the Dukes' first game of the year against Baltimore's Wheeling farm club. A few minutes before game time, Willy chatted with Henry Mullins, who took Willy long in San Juan, but now seemed like an old friend.

A few thousand enthusiastic but polite spectators at the small and well-kept park watched the Dukes manufacture a three-run lead for Laddy, who gave up five hits and no runs until the eighth. Strick, the closer-in-training, pitched the bottom of the ninth. Henry Mullins, who skulked to the plate and struck out three times in the game, took two quick strikes. Willy leaned over to Dan, kneeling next to her in the dugout, to check the time on his wristwatch and heard him exclaim, "Oh, Henry!" She looked out onto the field in utterly silent disbelief as the ball hit by Mullins vanished into the night. A dejected Strick walked with wobbly legs to the Dukes' dugout, seeming to be on the crest of tears. He told

Dan, "Do you know what Mullins said to me? *'Time to go home!'* Do you believe it?"

Willy's first outing of the season was the next evening against the Wheels and it was one of the oddest games she would ever pitch. She walked five batters, four of them in the first five innings, and got herself into and out of two jams before giving up a hit. A walk and a stolen base in the first frame put a runner in scoring position for two seconds. The base stealer slid past the bag, turning Pigpen's late and wide throw into "nailed him!" In the second, another walker went to first on ball four, moved to second on a sacrifice bunt, and took third when Darnell blew an attempted shoe-string catch in short center. Willy put an end to the inning with her first strikeout in the Mid-Atlantic League on three low-and-away sliders. In the bottom half of the third, the Wheels hit back-to-back singles off Willy with one out, and then died as the next two batters, in turn, grounded to third and short. That was all the hitting for the Wheels on this night. With the Dukes up 3-0, Max gave Willy a boost with his smooth-as-silk catch of a fly ball on the run and beautifully turned throw to double-up the runner at second in the ninth.

Willy Beal's first official game in "organized baseball" was a two-hit shutout. Willy's mates and the spectators attributed her five bases on balls to opening-night jitters, but Dan was sure that she wasn't getting the close calls "in the black" from the home plate ump. Yet she worked through it without complaint and won the game, impressing her skipper with her poise.

Willy's new crib was a small condo with barely enough floor space in the kitchen to swing open the fridge without slamming into the sink, but unless the front office kicked her up to Jacksonville or down to Shreveport, this would be home until September. Her daily five-mile run brought her through Old Towne Alexandria at noon, where she mingled with the lunchtime crowd in a donut shop, sitting at a comfy corner table, sipping a glass of spring water, and people-watching. Willy Beal was just another young working woman in a baseball cap and jogging suit.

The ballpark in Alexandria was a modernistic but cozy 5,000-seater. The grandstand was Yuppie Heaven, where Mom stuffed a picnic basket and cooler only to have Dad buy the kids hot dogs, sodas, and ice cream bars designed to melt inside the wrapper. Teenagers swarmed the park on Friday nights, adding a hyperactive shriek to the roar of the crowd. For Willy to slip in and out of the park unnoticed was impossible. Willy's groupies—consisting mostly of jiggly kids under ten, their forty-something moms, teens, and tweens of both genders—hovered at the service gate, lined up by the clubhouse door, and clustered around the dugout.

Willy's second appearance was at home against Philly's Wilmington Dels, who knocked one base hit off her in the second inning. Not another Del reached base until the seventh when Willy walked the lead-off batter. There was no complaint from Dan. Tonight the man in blue was calling strikes when Willy hit the black. Her "mistake" was erased when Pigpen caught the Del attempting to swipe second. This time the Dukes' catcher did it with a good throw. That proved crucial only moments later, as Wilmington's next batsman jumped on a sidearm curveball for a long single, which would have driven home the now-scratched runner from second. The Psycho, playing third base, made a falling dive to his right to snare a solidly hit liner to finish the inning. "High fives, low fives, and shakes all around!" Willy shouted. In the seventh, with a 2-0 lead, Darnell stood on third after a crowd-rousing triple, but the Dukes wasted a chance to score. In the eighth, Willy's second walk of the game preceded a pinch-hit triple off the right field wall, making the score 2-1. *Who's that guy?* wondered Willy. Nobody knew. The scoreboard read: Beaumont Teague. Willy struck out the next batter—fastball, curve, fastball, and goodbye—with the potential tying run on base. Willy completed her second winning performance by retiring the last three Dels on ground balls.Next came a road trip, kicking off in Schenectady, where Willy didn't pitch, followed by a weekend in Wilmington where she started the first game of an old-fashioned Sunday double-header against the Dels. The Dukes scored four runs in the first three innings. Max reached base on a walk, swiped second, and scored as his attempted theft of third led to a wild throw into left field from the Del's catcher. "Ichiro Street" was what the Psycho dubbed his peep, Max. The Dukes added two more in the third, but Willy ran into trouble that same inning, giving up a base hit to the lead-off batter, followed by a sacrifice bunt, advancing the runner to second. Next up was the same guy who pinch-hit the triple in last week's game with the Dels.

"So, who is he?"

"Beaumont Teague," advised Dan, "signed as a minor league free-agent after bein' released by Anaheim."

"We saw him with Tulsa when I was at Shreveport," commented Pigpen. "He can't run, can't field, got no arm, and can't hit a curve."

"Good!" said Willy. "That's what I'll throw him." She did and Teague slapped it to the opposite field for an RBI single. "I hope you're not planning on a career as a scout, John." The catcher shrugged and spat.

The Dukes went ahead 6-1 and Willy worked her way out

of jams with Dels on base in the fifth and sixth. She chalked up six strikeouts against seven hits and no walks for her third win of the season. For good measure, Beaumont Teague bounced out and whiffed in his second and third times at bat. She thus cut his batting average against her to .500!

In the second game of the twin bill, Laddy blanked the Dels until the eighth, when they rallied to tally three runs. With the Dukes leading by two, Wilmington loaded the bases with two outs and Strick came in to face Big Old Beau, once again pinch-hitting. A grand slam home run turned what should have been a save for Strickland into a loss for Zanetsky. "There's gonna be some bad blood there," Dan worried. Although Strick came back to nail down a save the next night, he was transferred to the Shreveport Gems by the front office. Officially, the move wasn't a demotion *per se*, but a therapeutic change of scenery.

The Schenectady Skylarks came to Alexandria and Willy took the mound on Wednesday night. Uncharacteristically, Willy allowed the first two batters of the game to reach base via a single and a walk. She set down the side without a run scoring, but was not so lucky in the second, when a single with two on and two out put the Skylarks ahead, 2-0. The familiar name of Mike Staczewski fairly jumped off the Toronto farm team's line-up card, his father and namesake being a former big league batting champ. When Stash the Younger knelt in the on-deck circle, Willy called time and ran over to him, shouting and bouncing. "Hey, you're Stash's kid, Mike Jr., right?" She shook his hand and yelled, "This is so cool! I'm a second-generation ballplayer, too, you know." She shook his hand again with a comically exaggerated pumping motion and yelped, "Awesome!" When Junior Stash came to bat, the fearsome woman with the wicked slider gave him a cutesy wave and chirped, "Hi, Mike!"

"She's a nut case," said a sub on the Skylark bench.

"Oh, yeah?" said his skipper. "Watch her."

Willy sidearmed a slider on the right-hand corner, sidearmed another on the left-hand corner, and fired an overhand fastball that he swung on and missed. "Hey, see you later, Mike! Nice to meet you!"

A run in the sixth and the seventh brought the Dukes back. Willy's mates then exploded with four home runs in the eighth inning, three of them in succession, five in all in the game, which ended up an 8-2 laugher. Trailing most of the way, Willy threw much harder than in her previous three starts, using more fastballs, whipping the slider exclusively sidearm to bring it to the plate a shade faster, and slipping in her curve as a change of pace instead of the cutter because Pigpen had great difficulty catching the ball as it rose and trailed inward to righty hitters. Willy fanned ten, her highest count of kays to date, and walked three, but held the Skylarks to six hits in notching her fourth win, still without a loss.

After cracking one of the Dukes' five homers, giving him three in two days and putting his average over .300, Pigpen Pantagones was unexpectedly brought up to the Diamonds. Dan was mildly amused. "He's what they were lookin' for," he said. "They need a backup that can hit. I guess Cello can't catch all nine innings for 162 games."

However, Psycho Bielski was enraged. "That fathead gets a couple lucky shots and he's a Diamond! I bust my chops and I'm still sittin' here."

"Yeah, and what about me?" asked Max, trying to calm Psycho. "I'm hittin' .333."

"Okay, I hear ya, bro'! It sucks, Max! The first move was supposed to be me, you, or Darnell, not freakin' Pigpen." In short order, Psycho was frothing at the mouth. Dan expected

Bielski to tear up the clubhouse.

"I'm gonna recommend that the front office bump him up to Triple-A so I can get some peace and quiet around here. That kid's a maniac!" However, the powers-that-be weren't ready to move Psycho Bielski, a disappointment of equal weight to both player and manager.

Chapter 14

Samantha Khoury, a staff writer for *Sportsworld* magazine, impatiently tapped her keys against the vinyl dashboard of her car parked outside the Capital Center in Landover, Maryland, waiting for her editor in New York to come on the line. Her boss's voice rumbled to life.

"What's up?" she asked in her usually clipped manner.

"Sam, I want you to hop over to Alexandria and get a story on the female pitcher, Willy Beal."

"Lonnie, we have hockey and basketball playoffs and you want me to cover minor league baseball? I don't *do* minor league baseball."

"That's all well and good, but it looks like she's for real," said Lonnie. "She's out of the two-headed-calf and man-bites-dog category now. She's already the top pitcher in the league and no one expects her to stay down there for very long."

"Do you want me to do a profile?" Sam asked.

"Yes," answered Len. "I need four or five pages for next week."

"Why is she *my* assignment?"

"Why do you think, Sam?"

"Oh," she mocked ruefully. "Could it be the woman's angle?"

"And you're so darn good, Sam," Lonnie teased.

"Yeah, sure, I love you, too, Lonnie."

"Well, whatever," croaked the senior editor, now sounding distracted, telling Sam Khoury the time had come to hang up and get to work, or, more appropriately, off his mind.

"Bye!" She tossed her cell phone onto the passenger's seat with a hatchetlike throw. "Jerk!"

Sam arranged to meet Willy at her condo after the Dukes' game with the Johnstown Flood two nights later. The two women talked while seated on the carpeted floor. The female ballplayer assumed the lotus position, while Sam's left leg was bent to prop a yellow lined notepad and her head leaned on her right elbow, planted on the coffee table, where she put her tape recorder and lap-top computer.

"Does this thing bother you?" Sam asked as she popped a teeny cassette into the pocket-sized recorder.

"I've seen such devices before," Willy replied with a slight, inscrutable grin.

Sam was surprised at how quiet, still, and serene Willy seemed, barely moving a muscle, except for her mouth to speak. "Soft and controlled" was the description that came to mind.

Willy began, "I don't think it should be all that surprising if the first woman in the majors is a pitcher." She spoke in an unexpectedly gentle whisper, but her eyes locked on Sam's, even following such incidental actions as the movement of her pen and playing with the split ends of her stringy brown hair. "I always thought of pitching as being kind of a *female* role in the game," Willy said.

"By analogy, of course," offered Sam.

"Sure, I don't think some of the big studs on the New York Diamonds would agree," laughed Willy.

"At least, not without a fight."

"Well, you know how fragile male egos can be, but, actually, they're all really great guys."

"Even Jacobson?" Sam asked suggestively.

"I didn't get to know Jake all that well in the spring. So, I can't really say," responded Willy. Then she said, "You're not gonna print all this, are you?"

Sam stopped the tape recorder and promised, "I'll leave out the comments about studs and male egos."

"Okay," Willy mouthed delicately, resuming her studied composure.

"Go on with what you started to say about the pitcher's female role."

"Baseball is the only sport where the *defense* holds the ball. Pitching is such an active, aggressive form of defense that it seems like an offensive position, but it's still defensive. The pitcher carries the *seed* of the game in her hands." Willy cupped her hands as if holding a ball. "She brings forth the seed and *delivers* it into play." She extended her hands outward, before slowly drawing them back to her breast. "All *life* in the game stems from the pitcher's hand. The *fruit* of the game comes from the pitcher delivering her pitch and she *bears* the burden of winning or losing the game." Momentarily transfixed by Willy's fluid gesturing of arms and hands, Sam felt as if she were watching an interpretive dance. "But, then again," Willy continued, "if you look at the pitcher-catcher relationship, it's the pitcher who plays the *masculine* role. The catcher is the *feminine* receptacle, superficially passive, openly waiting to *receive* the seed from the pitcher, but also the one who *protects* the pitcher, *nurtures* the pitcher, and stays at *home* to guard it by laying down her own body." Willy paused and smiled, her brown eyes open wide and sparkling as she said, "And they do it face to face!"

"This is great stuff," gurgled Sam, as she scribbled on her notepad.

"What's so funny?" Willy asked uncertainly.

"I came here expecting to find a gum-chewing, fast-talking, slow-witted jockette and instead I'm getting psychosexual masculine-feminine metaphors about baseball."

"Do you wanna talk about Near Eastern and East Asian philosophy and mysticism?"

"Maybe next time!" Sam quipped. Then she asked, "What about other sports?"

"I enjoy other sports, track and field, especially. Of course, I played a lot of basketball and soccer. I like rugby, lacrosse, field hockey, and ice hockey because, like baseball, you can be normal size and still play, but they're all pretty much the same basic game in principle when you think about it."

Sam arched her eyebrows with exaggerated curiosity. "What's that about *normal size*?"

"I'm normal." Willy tilted her head a shade to smile. "Just tall, that's all."

"What about football?" asked Sam, expecting Willy to say something along the lines of "Yeah, it's okay, or no it's not my cup of tea."

"Actually, my biggest issue with football was figuring out if I should be a running back, wide receiver, or the Q.B."

For a moment, Sam stepped out of her wag's skin and moved her face intimately close to Willy's, proposing, "Why not all three?" *And I think she could do it all the way to the Stupor Bowl, to boot!* Shifting gears with calculated ease, Sam asked

Willy, "Are you a Buddhist?"

"No, not really. I got into Buddhism . . . Zen mostly . . . and Taoism and Hinduism through yoga and meditation, which are part of my mental and physical regimen, just like aerobics and running a few miles. Buddhism is as much of a discipline and a philosophy as a theology."

"Aren't there many different branches of Buddhism and can't you combine elements of Buddhism with other religions?"

"Of course, as the Dalai Lama says: 'Whatever you believe, believe it.'"

Of course, she says!

"I went on a retreat one summer. Buddha camp!" Willy disclosed easily. "But I found it took a level of devotion and self-denial I wasn't ready for."

When Samantha Khoury first introduced herself to Willy, she jabbered in double negatives and disjointed Stengelese syntax with her pals on the Dukes. Since their interview began, however, she articulated only carefully constructed phrases. *Who is the real Willy Beal?*

The interviewer worked her subject in the same fashion as Willy pitched to a batter. Sam set her up to throw her a curve: "Are you a cream-filled chocolate sandwich cookie?"

"Are you a jelly donut?" Willy giggled in response as if she were flicking off a foul tip.

"I think you know what I mean," Sam asserted.

"Yeah, I do. I'm just Willy," she said, spreading her arms and "giving face" as if she were on camera. "I'm not a novelty act or a freak of nature and I'm not a male trapped inside a female's body, either."

"Why do you fluff off questions about your personal life?" Sam asked casually.

Willy leaned closer to Sam and asked, "Why do you crinkle your forehead and scrunch up your nose when you ask a question?"

Sam twisted and contorted her facial features even more and replied in a delayed return gesture, "I don't know. *Ha-ha-ha!*"

Willy looked at the digital camera among the several pieces of baggage that Sam brought with her, asking, "Are we gonna take some pictures?"

Sam nodded and groaned slightly as she unbent her legs to reach for the camera. "I picked up some publicity shots from the team's web site, but I'd rather have fresh, new pix. If you want, you can go change into a uniform."

"Let's do it in sweats," Willy said excitedly. "I have a new set, light blue with white stripes."

Sam said, "Sure, why not?" and Willy went upstairs. *Why show you in a uniform that says "Dukes" when you may be wearing one that says "Diamonds" soon enough? Isn't that right, Willy?*

After Sam snapped a dozen photos of Willy, they moved to the kitchen table and schmoozed over herbal tea, strawberries, and bananas.

"No coffee!" Sam exclaimed initially. "Not even decaf?" Sam made a sour face, picked up a banana, ripped away the peel, and bit off the top with a lusty click of her teeth. "Argh!" Willy and Sam talked about sports, life, death, and the universe for another hour and a half. "It's one o'clock!" shouted Sam, startled at the realization. "I have to be up by noon, anyway. I'll be, like, totally fried."

"Now I know why they call y'all wags!" Willy mused.

"You can dish out the chatter pretty well yourself, pal." Sam gave Willy her business card with her e-mail, fax, voice, and cell phone numbers. Then Willy sent Samantha Khoury on her way with an unexpectedly affectionate farewell hug.

Just before Willy's next scheduled start, Dan noticed that she seemed sluggish during her pregame workout. "Ya look a little peaked, Willy." Dan asked, "Are ya sure ya can pitch tonight?"

"It's only a little headache," she answered. "It'll pass."

Lew Shankleton made his first trip to Alexandria to observe the progress of the Dukes' pitchers. Dan and Shanks found Willy sitting on the locker room floor in the lotus position with her eyes closed, methodically rubbing her temples. "Listen," Dan said as her eyes popped open. "Let's forget tonight. I'll tell Zanetsky to get warmed up."

"No, Dan," protested Willy. "I just had some celery and pineapple juice with quinine. I'll be okay. Shanks, you're here and everything."

"I can watch ya tomorrow night," insisted Shanks. "I need to see Laddy, too. We want ya at a hundred percent."

"You're scratched, Willy!" declared the skipper.

When Willy took a seat on the bench instead of her spot at the rubber, Max asked, "What's the matter? Ya got the cramps or somethin'?"

"Shush!" said Willy, whipping his chin with the leafy end of a celery stalk on which she was chewing.

The next night's crowd swelled to standing-room-only because of a freebie ticket giveaway, a big local promotion on Sebastian Fabian's pop music radio station in Fairfax County. Willy was besieged by moonstruck male and hero-worshiping female teenagers, dangerously overpopulating the galleries, alongside hundreds of smaller kids, wearing—to Willy's amazement—tee shirts picturing a cartoonish caricature in pigtails.

"I believe the contemporary terminology is 'test marketing.' We are a test market," Dan advised, "for Willy Beal!"

As should be no surprise to anyone following the Mid-Atlantic League, Beaumont Teague was now the Dels' regular left fielder and number three hitter. Big Ugly Beau and the Dels' clean-up batter, Leon Bowdry, socked back-to-back doubles off Willy in the first inning, putting a 1-0 lead on the boards. Willy gave up only three more hits over the next seven frames. In the home eighth, a single and homer put Willy and the Dukes on top, 2-1. In the ninth, Willy was again to face the Dels' two best hitters. Beau grounded out and Leon popped up to Psycho in foul territory by third base. With two outs, the suburban Beltway crowd rose as one, chanting Willy's name. She pranced about the mound, pumped her fist in the air, and set her pigtails swirling between pitches to the would-be third out standing at the plate. *"Wil-lee! Wil-lee!"* Willy's antics became more spirited and the fans' delight heightened with each pitch. Dan wondered whether she deliberately threw three balls away from the hitter to prolong the drama. With a full count, she spun a screwball overhand, expecting the Del to swing wildly as the pitch dropped in front of him. He held his bat in check and took ball four. *"Aww!"* Willy's legion of disappointed admirers sighed. Willy screamed, shook her fist at the runner on first, and pointed her finger at the next batter, who hit a slow roller back to the mound. Willy spun on her heels, gave a high and wide kick of her leg, and fired the ball to second base for the game-ending out.

"Who's the girl, Max?"

"You're the girl, Willy!"

Slap! Tap! Bump! Bump!

"A nifty five-hitter," Shanks told Manny Gabriel. The Greek nodded. "The Wilmington kid pitched a two-hitter for crissakes and nobody gives a hoot. She didn't just *win* the game, she *owned* it."

"How's it feel to be the George Digby of the new millennium?" Shanks asked, referring to the scout who signed a skinny kid from 'Bama named Hank Aaron to his first professional contract.

Gabriel sat upright and folded his thick arms across his chest, shivering with laughter. "Fabian said, 'I want her! She's mine!' If I'd let her get away, he would've canned me."

Shanks grinned and punched the scout's arm in slow motion. "But it feels good, don't it?"

"Bet your butt it does, Lew!"

The morning after, the Alexandria Dukes awoke to the news that Laddy was going to AAA Jacksonville to replace Jay Phillips, who was called up to the big club. After two starting assignments and two losses, Jay was returned to the Jewels and Laddy got the call, but it turned out to be a temporary measure. He pitched one game, going five innings for no decision, and was sent back to AAA. The Diamonds were coping by using Zinger as a starter, thus depleting the bullpen. Brooks and Langevin were working for two or three innings instead of three or four outs at a time. The solution was to bring up Todd Strickland from AA Shreveport. "The revolvin' door is spinnin' outta control!" pronounced Dan Blanchard on the hot, cramped, and foul-smelling bus ride to Bradford, Pennsylvania.

An advance copy of *Sportsworld* came in the mail only a few days after Willy's interview with Samantha Khoury. Due to the mild case of mediaphobia that Willy picked up from spring training, she feared lamentable misquotes and comments out of context. The first line of the article was its title: *"There's never been a pitcher like Willy Beal before!"* The text was blocked off in large white letters against a full-color photo of Willy simulating her pitching motion, wearing her blue and white sweatsuit. Willy spread out on the floor to read what Sam had written, jiggling her foot and gently rolling her tongue between her front teeth, savoring every delectable word. "Her first language—her mother tongue—is baseball. Its jargon comes naturally to her and she easily applies its truisms to the world at large." Sam quoted Willy's sexual analogies about the pitcher's and catcher's roles and called her "a tireless practitioner and student of the science of pitching." At the end, Sam Khoury editorialized: "Even if this intelligent and flamboyant player fails to become Big League Baseball's first show girl, Willy Beal is special."

Alone in her room, Willy whispered, "Hey, Sam, thanks!"

The crowds surrounding Willy thickened and prolonged her departure from the field after games, even when she wasn't pitching. The new issue of *Sportsworld* hit the newsstands and set off a most unwelcome disruption as a horde of folks waited for Willy to make her noon-hour pit stop at the little coffee shop with copies of the magazine for her to autograph.

Art Ridzik finally resurfaced. He set up shop in a nearby motel and gave Willy a two-week itinerary with at least one or sometimes two promotional appearances each day. After a balloon and popcorn studded visit to a DC daycare center, Willy said to Artie, "I don't believe this! All those little peanuts know who I am. Not one of them is more than five years old."

"I suppose you haven't noticed yet that you're famous."

Amid the activity and attention whirling around, Willy was having the time of her life. Yet she kept her mind on the business at hand.

Willy started off her fourth game against Wilmington with a blistering three-pitch strikeout, but found herself being challenged by the Dels all the way. Beaumont Teague continued to be a nuisance, doubling in the first, singling in the fourth, and singling again in the sixth. Dan was as close as he could be to pulling Willy out of the game. In the ninth, the Dels put runners on second and third with none out. Now Willy faced not only leaving the game, but losing it. She drew an infield pop-up and a soft line drive to left before nailing the final out with a grounder to Psycho at third. The crowd of 8,000—the largest to attend a game this year in Delaware—turned out to see the female phenom and gave her a loud and long ovation when she ran off the field victorious. Willy won her second shutout and was still undefeated at 6-0.

"Why didn't you take me out of there?" Willy asked her skipper after the game.

Dan yanked a thumb over his shoulder toward the audience with a jolly chuckle. "That mob of yuppies and their puppies would've had my hide if I did."

Four days later, at home against Wheeling, Willy's seventh game was carried on local radio, television, and cable. Not an empty seat was to be had as kids came in by the busload. There were boxes full of the silly Willy tee shirts and shrill prepubescent squeals of *"Wil-lee! Wil-lee!"*

On this summerlike afternoon, the Dukes scored a run in the third on Darnell's RBI double, but Willy surrendered a triple with one out in the fourth, followed by a long sac fly to left off the bat of "Oh, Henry" Mullins, the ball hit sufficiently deep to allow the Wheel on third base to tag up, score, and tie the game. The Dukes opened up a 4-1 lead with three runs in the bottom of the fourth and no other Wheels reached base for the rest of the game. Willy set down the last seventeen batters in a row. The final act was another theatrically delivered game-ending strikeout. Willy's pulse rate, body temperature, and adrenaline were sky-high as fans swarmed her for autographs, handshakes, and touching—anywhere on her person seemed to be fair territory. The circuslike atmosphere surrounding her immediately segued into a postgame press conference in the clubhouse for the bevy of out-of-town wags. Willy conducted her media fest in the crowded clubhouse in Alexandria by sitting on a tabletop, sipping tomato juice with lemon, celery, and pepper, surrounded by the gathered scribes. After being redundantly and persistently asked the same old question, "How does it feel?"

Willy stated succinctly, "I'm not a female pitcher. There's no such thing as pitching female. I'm a pitcher who's female," all the while smiling radiantly.

Nine hard-pitched innings followed by the press conference got the better of Willy. She slept halfway through the next morning, arose to breakfast and exercise, and went back to bed at noon. She got up to stay at three o'clock, watched some tube, ate three apples, and essentially recovered her normal self in time for the Dukes' game versus the Skylarks. Willy arrived at the ballpark wearing purple shorts over a pink leotard and a new pair of white clogs. There was a hoot from Psycho, a whistle from Max, a "Shush!" from Willy, and a call of beckoning from Dan. "What is it, skipper?" She stood in the doorway, holding her head high, which Dan found pleasing. Willy was gently bobbing on the soles of her clogs. He motioned for her to enter his office. As she closed the door, she saw a look of unhappiness in her manager's eyes.

"Something wrong, Dan?"

He shook his head as he announced somberly, "The front

office called . . . " Willy felt a tingle of excitation as the surge of blood quickened in her veins. "They're shippin' ya out."

"Jacksonville?" she asked in a frail voice, her hands visibly shaking.

Dan said no. Willy covered her face. As the adrenaline rushed, she stiffened her spine and limbs to hold fast. He said, "New York," and she gasped.

Willy sobbed and giggled simultaneously, while Dan pawed clumsily through the mess on his desk in quest of a box of tissues. He tentatively placed his hand on her shoulder as she wiped, patted, and blew.

"I don't believe this is really happening, Dan." His hand now grew warmer and more comfortable, and he gently stroked her shoulder. Willy looked at him, almost imploringly, "Is it for real?" Dan thought she had never seemed so pure, so innocent, or so young, although she was the oldest player on his team.

"Listen, Willy," he said, trying to sound stern. "I'm none too happy about it. I could've won a pennant here this season, but I can't make it without ya."

"Sor-ry!" she said with a smile and a sniffle.

"And I'm gonna miss ya."

Nice move, Dan! He said to himself: *Now she's bawling out loud.* Dan guided her toward the couch with his arms wrapped around her. Seated together, she wanted only to hug and slobber on his collar and that suited him just fine.

"A lotta kids come and go. Some make it, some don't, but once in a while a gem comes along. You're a gem, Willy."

She pressed her soft lips to his stubbled cheek. He gave her a quick smacking kiss in return and she asked, "What do I do now?"

"Ya can hang around for the game, but ya probably wanna

pack. Ya should call your mother, ya know."

"I'll wanna say goodbye to the guys, too," said Willy as she rubbed her eyes with a balled up tissue. She was no longer crying, but shivering uncontrollably.

"Right," said Dan. "Then call Kristin Tracy in New York. Remember her? She's in charge of player personnel. She's a sharp cookie, not like some of the other numb-skulls that work for Fabian."

Kristin told Willy, "We'll fly you into Newark on the shuttle. It's less than a one-hour flight. Take a cab right to the Meadowlands." Kristin continued in her businesslike way while Willy listened wordlessly. "We'll put you up in a motel near the stadium until you get your bearings. Anything else I can do?"

"Yeah, if this is a dream, don't wake me up."

"Gotcha," the director of player personnel laughed lightly.

To be continued . . .

Acknowledgments

The author wishes to thank Marilyn Cohen (No Girls in the Clubhouse), Bill Littlefield (Only A Game), and Elinor Nauen (Diamonds Are A Girl's Best Friend) for reading and commenting on the manuscript. Likewise, thanks to my best buds, Mike Rodericks and Marcie Seigal. Above all, I thank my wife and soul-mate, Jane Mitchell, who never needed to read the book because she was the first to hear Willy's story.

About the Author

Dennis N. Ricci is a writer, historian, and political scientist living in Massachusetts. A lifelong baseball aficionado and amateur sabremetrician, Mr. Ricci is a die-hard fan of the Boston Red Sox, Brooklyn Dodgers, and Kansas City Monarchs.